Praise for
The Winning *Spirit* -
Building Employee Enthusiasm

"Lisa Wicker's theory on the human spirit and its role in winning goes to the core of success in life. The book is not just for employers and employees, but for all who wish to attain and sustain success in the enterprise of life. It is admirable that the author invites the reader to engage in meaningful self-analysis."

Thelma B. Thompson, Ph.D., president
University of Maryland Eastern Shore

"Lisa Wicker has always been an inspiration to all who have been around her. Everyone who reads her book will not only be encouraged to do more with their life, but be inspired to take on the challenges of everyday situations head to head."

Greg Russell
The Movie Show Plus, Detroit, Michigan

"Lisa Lindsay Wicker's book gives examples of **"The Winning Spirit**"...while building employee enthusiasm. The greater the excitement in one's career, the greater the chances for success through a positive attitude which leads to more leadership opportunities. In "The Winning Spirit," Wicker shows you how to use that spirit to inspire people to greater success. A 'must have' book for business owners, managers and employees alike."

Edward Deeb, president & CEO
Michigan Business and Professional Association

" Just when we think corporate America has lost it's conscience and energy, Lisa Wicker reminds us how to rekindle a blend of values, integrity and spiritual foundation to unleash the strongest force — and that is employee enthusiasm. Her book flows with vivid interest as she weaves in her own experiences to anchor her concepts in realness. She challenges the reader to experience the power of being accountable. An exciting and eager read, Lisa reveals how a strong leader can liberate that inner fire in their people. The action-based exercises beckon the reader to apply successful concepts in their own life…my spirit was refreshed and uplifted by her gifted work."

Sidney R. Bonvallet, president
Fresh Horizons, Farmington Hills, Michigan

"Ms. Wicker provides such wonderful insight on today's workforce and what we can do to change attitudes. It's amazing the power of positive influences that leaders have and their powerful impact on the success of business. Ms. Wicker is to be commended for addressing the 'soft' people issues that everyone else has ignored for years."

Jennifer Kluge, publisher
Corp! Magazine

"In a time when job security is a figment of ones imagination, in a time when ones strong work-ethics have taken a back seat to the possibility of corporate down-sizing, and in a time when job outsourcing to foreign lands is the new normal, Lisa Wicker presents personal history lessons and practical wisdom for maintaining enthusiasm about the jobs with which we have been blessed. May all employees who struggle with an inability to remain excited about their employment, and may all employers who are challenged with sustaining employee morale, be restored, renewed, and refreshed with the spiritual golden nuggets for work success as manifested within the pages of Ms. Wicker's debut-must read."

Minister Beverly (Coleman) Alexander, M.A
Author of "Pressing Pass the Mess to Receive God's Best"

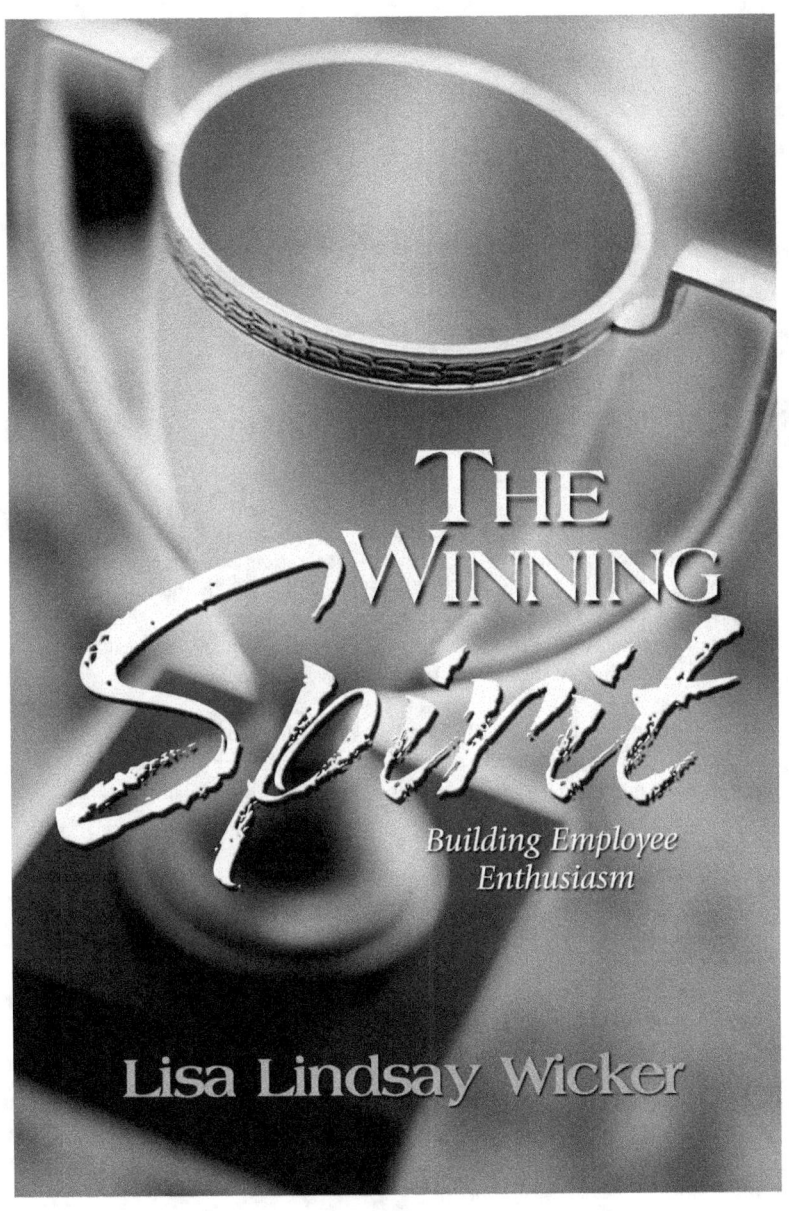

THE WINNING *Spirit*

Building Employee Enthusiasm

Lisa Lindsay Wicker

Winning Spirit Ministries • Rochester, Michigan

Dedication

This book is dedicated with love to my husband, Michael, my friend, partner and soul mate. Thank you for caring and for being a wonderful husband and father.

To my sons Justin and Jonathan, whom I love dearly and who have been wonderful blessings in my life. I feel so fortunate to have you both as sons. You are winners!

Acknowledgements

- To "Mama," Laverne Gardner Lindsay Stewart, for always being there with a listening ear, encouragement, love and friendship.
- To my sisters and brother – Dr. Tamara Lindsay Roberts, Teri Lindsay Fobbs, Brenda Lindsay Estes and Louie Lindsay Jr. – for always keeping me in your prayers and providing the constant spirit of humor, love and sharing within our family.
- To my late grandparents, Mr. & Mrs. John Clarence Gardner Sr., for their devotion, love and guidance to reach for the best.
- To my late Aunt Carolyn Moore, our spiritual guide, who made sure our family knew the teachings of God.
- To Uncle John Gardner, who taught each of us to share and who has always been our star.
- To Aunt Gay Gladney, the love of my life and a solid example of grace and poise.
- To my cousins - Gay Marie Gladney, Charles Gladney, Fred Gladney, Jaqueline Gladney, Clyde Moore Jr., William Tyree Moore, Myrna Moore Harris and Tawnya Moore McGee: I love you.
- To my nieces and nephews: I love you too!
- To my Lydia Circle prayer partners for your faithful prayers and encouragement.

A special 'Thank You' to: Mintzi Schramm, Ph.D., for her patience, guidance, and editorial expertise, Christine Ladd for her assistance, the late Sharon Bullock for her support and enthusiasm about the project, LaTanya Orr for her prayers and patience to hang in there with me and for her graphics and layout talent, and Linda Angér for her guidance and eye for excellence. In addition, I thank the following friends and colleagues who read drafts of the manuscript and gave me insight: Bill Cheek, J. T. Battenberg, Aubrey Lee, Bill Tate, and Karen Sanford, and to my most Higher Power, the Lord Jesus Christ – to Him I give the glory!

Contents

Preface

The stimulus to write the book came in 1997. At that time, I had no idea what steps were required to share my knowledge, inspiration and personal viewpoint on the subject of leadership and employee enthusiasm. As the vision and spiritual stirrings took shape in my soul, I wrote my thoughts and ideas out longhand. In fact, the ideas came almost effortless onto the pages, daily. I knew instantly that the plan for this book was ordained spiritually. So, in 1998, when I was asked to take on the role of leading the initiative on Employee Enthusiasm at one of the world's largest organizations, I knew that the universe had lined up perfectly for this very moment.

This book is a personal account of who I am and what leadership means to me. The principles discussed relate to God as a Principal in the development of leadership, managerial skill and motivation. While this is true in my life and in the lives of many leaders, I know that it is not necessarily a conscious factor for some great leaders, nor is it consciously considered in many successful businesses.

I could have easily omitted reference to God in the interest of heightening corporate attention. I've chosen, instead, to present the material as it was given to me spiritually, and to convey what I feel as authentically as possible.

A good leader is key to building and sustaining a successful company, church, university, and even a family. I believe that good leaders aren't necessarily born that way. Some of the best became leaders because of their desire for excellence, and because someone nurtured and helped develop their leadership potential.

Being a good leader isn't easy. It is a tough assignment to be competent and fair while getting the job done. It is even tougher to be a leader who is a model. However, all who are in positions of authority need to take an honest look at their style and the impact it may have on others. Like it or not, we are watched daily by the words we speak, the dispositions we share, the clarity we bring, the competence and skill-set we possess, and the judgment we choose. Each of us exemplifies leadership, whether in the church, the workplace, or the home. The ability to influence a positive future for those under our authority helps shape people to be their best, so that they produce, contribute, and feel good about being a part of the organization and the people they are around.

I trust you will use the practical knowledge and thoughts you gain from this book and use it in your daily lives, and that as a result, you and the people you work with or live with will create and enjoy more productive lives.

— *Lisa J. Lindsay Wicker*

How to Use this Book

Each chapter of this book covers a specific principle inherent in *The Winning Spirit*.

Following the chapter text, there is a case illustration showing the principle in action, and power tools – a selection of scriptural reflections included to enhance your leadership skills on your journey to a Winning Spirit. Each chapter ends with an exercise – four self-analysis questions designed to help you identify your strengths, and areas of growth opportunity.

I hope that you will enjoy building employee enthusiasm as much as I do!

CHAPTER ONE

The Winning Spirit

LIFE IS NO BRIEF CANDLE TO ME. IT IS A
SORT OF SPLENDID TORCH WHICH I HAVE
HOLD OF FOR THE MOMENT.
George Bernard Shaw

During 20 years of work experience, I've learned much about people. I've discovered the amazing difference leadership can make in any organization. How a leader treat their people can mean the ultimate success or failure of that organization.

As I write, I remember the leaders I have known — people with winning spirits — and the valuable lessons I learned from them. This book distills these experiences into leadership lessons. I hope that by reading these pages you too will embrace these leadership qualities and make them your own.

HOW LEADERS TREAT THEIR PEOPLE CAN MEAN THE ULTIMATE SUCCESS OR FAILURE OF THAT ORGANIZATION.

My best leadership models were my mother and grandparents. Through example, they taught me to develop a winning spirit by being enthusiastic about life.

Growing up in Mississippi, I learned early on that "things" do not inspire enthusiasm. A spiritual, rich life is not based on material wealth. Although I was a child in the '60s — an African-American child in an age when segregated public restrooms, restaurants and buses were still the norm — I lived a simple but good life with my family. My parents were divorced; mother, my siblings and I lived with my grandparents. We didn't have a car. We walked or took a taxi wherever we needed to go. My mom had a high school education and worked at a hospital as an X-ray technician.

You can well imagine some of the trying moments I had growing up in the Mississippi Delta back in those days, dealing with the day-to-day reality of "separate but equal."

When I look back, I don't dwell on what I didn't have. I remember instead my very rich upbringing. I was raised by my mom, my grandparents, the neighbor across the street, my mother's sister across town, and by the entire church family. A majority of the teachers at my school also went to my church. There was family everywhere I turned, and no getting around good behavior and the basic values of life. As a result, all four of my siblings and I went to college and earned a bachelor's degree or higher.

The race riots weigh heavy in my memory, but I also remember how my family framed the riot scene with love rather than fear. We knew who and what we were in terms of the world. While

I certainly recall walking to the neighborhood store and having people call me names, I also was blessed to make lifelong friendships as a result of school integration. Because ours is a diverse world, I believe that integration prepared me well for life.

The message I got from my folks and my extended family is that success comes from keeping God at the center of your life and treating people with dignity and respect. I was taught to believe in myself and to know that with God all things are possible. I was taught to never let anyone limit, undermine, or define me solely by my race.

I can truly say that my success as an adult is based upon understanding and firmly believing that all of us are created in the image of God and that His spirit is what energizes and inspires us toward extraordinary success.

My folks were true leaders. For me, my four siblings and cousins – who lived across town – the torch they passed on is the fire we carry within us today. They taught us to look within ourselves for meaning, to be accepting and nonjudgmental, to live every moment with hope, and to dream and aspire to excellence in all that we do. They demonstrated that a *Winning Spirit* is first grown inside of us, long before it is visible to others.

I pass their torch, in turn, to you through this message of enthusiasm. Accept this torch and the responsibility you have to be the best you can be, and to inspire others through your enthusiasm to achieve their highest aspirations.

CASE ILLUSTRATION
Paul Fought to Win People

We read in the scriptures that Paul used his convictions to build bridges for people to win, not walls that they could not climb over. His one great desire was to win the lost, which was a factor in all his decisions.

During his ministry to the church at Corinth, Paul explains his beliefs and methods for reaching the unsaved. Though the church was in Corinth, he knew that Corinth was also in the church; he knew that quarrelling and divisiveness had erupted among the Corinthians, infecting the fellowship and witness of the Christian congregation. Paul moved about Corinth, setting forth godly guidelines for conduct consistent with the grace of God.

Paul knew that the church wouldn't ever be perfect, just as we, as leaders, know that work environments, families, and professional organizations aren't perfect. Like Paul, we as leaders must recognize and utilize the gifts and strengths of the people around us. Like Paul, we must fight to win people. Paul writes:

> *To the weak I became weak, that I might win*
> *the weak; I have become all things to all men,*
> *that I may by all means save some.*
> (1 Corinthians 9-22)

POWER TOOLS

*Clothe yourselves with
compassion, kindness, humility,
gentleness and patience...Over all
these virtues, put on love, which binds
them all together in perfect unity.*
(Colossians 3:12,14)

*Now the Lord is the Spirit, and
where the Spirit of the Lord is, there
is freedom. And we, who with unveiled
faces all reflect the Lord's glory, are
being transformed into His likeness
with ever-increasing glory, which comes
from the Lord, who is the Spirit.*
(2 Corinthians 3:17-18)

A happy heart makes the face cheerful.
(Proverbs 15:13)

But we have the mind of Christ.
(1 Corinthians 2:16)

CONSIDER THE TOPIC OF
"Displaying a Winning Spirit."

**ANSWER THE QUESTIONS BELOW TO ENHANCE
YOUR LEADERSHIP SKILLS.**

1. How does this characteristic show up in your life?

_____

_____

_____

2. What is it trying to reveal or teach you? What can you learn from it? What awareness does it trigger?

_____

_____

_____

3. How might you use this awareness to make positive changes in your life?

_____

_____

_____

4. Are you willing to live your life differently? In what way?

_____

_____

_____

CHAPTER TWO

The Source of Enthusiasm

THE SPIRIT OF A MAN IS THE LAMP OF THE LORD,
SEARCHING ALL THE INNER DEPTHS OF HIS HEART.
Proverbs 20:27

My work ethic didn't begin in the workplace. It began in my home, where I learned the Christian values that I hold in my heart. I believe this is how it works for everyone. People are motivated by the values they grew up with, and they bring these values to the workplace.

Nevertheless, others can, and do, inspire the values by which we live.

The leadership in an organization has a profound effect on encouraging or dampening people's natural enthusiasm.

THE LEADERSHIP IN AN ORGANIZATION HAS A PROFOUND EFFECT ON ENCOURAGING OR DAMPENING PEOPLE'S NATURAL ENTHUSIASM.

Time and again, I have seen how the climate of an organization mirrors the leadership and leader values.

Enthusiasm is natural. Just look at young children – they are naturally interested in their environment, eager to do a good job, and to please others. Most of us start a new job with similar enthusiasm and sparkling potential. We're excited about new opportunities to use our skills and to do our best to accomplish great things. That attitude probably helped us get hired for the job.

Yet, frequently, the enthusiasm and excitement of that first day on the job wore off. Why did we lose the zest and vigor to push forward in the cause and vision of the organization?

The answer almost certainly lies in how we're treated at work. If our natural creativity is stifled, we feel valueless. An organization's leadership must reinforce our worth and value by allowing creativity, rewarding innovation and embracing risk as a significant virtue.

The World Book encyclopedia defines *enthusiasm* as "zest, eagerness, vigor," and derives from the Greek word *enthous,* meaning, "inspired." Further research shows that the word *enthous* stems from the ancient Greek words, *theos,* which means "God," and *entos,* which means "within." Thus, in a literal sense, the word *enthusiasm* means "God's spirit within." It is God's spirit that enables us to function with enthusiasm. Just as a lamp reveals what is in the darkness, so too, God reveals what is in our hearts, our thoughts, our attitudes, our desires and our will. God is the spirit who energizes us and provides the inspiration for excellence. Once you understand that God's spirit is within, you can unlock the enthusiasm within.

So too must the culture and climate of an organization come from the heart, not from the head. While leadership may make an outward show of excitement and vigor in the form of company slogans, true enthusiasm comes from the soul of the organization — from leaders who generate enthusiasm and help staff reach their full potential.

We learn and benefit from each other. As the individual grows and achieves his or her personal goals, ultimately the organization grows and achieves its goals.

CASE ILLUSTRATION
How a Father's Dream Became a Son's Zest for Life

In September 2006, tens of thousands traveled to the Australian Zoo to memorialize and pay tribute to a man who allowed nothing to stand in the way of his enthusiasm and excitement for the natural world. Steve "Crocodile Hunter" Irwin was incredibly popular and touched the hearts of millions around the world in a very special way. An exuberant conservationist and television entertainer, he is remembered for his "great zest for life and enthusiasm" for the conservation of endangered animals. Described as a modern day Noah, he is credited with getting a whole new generation excited about wildlife. *Crocodile Hunter*, his television show, is seen in more than 60 million U.S. homes and more than 122 countries worldwide.

Steve's father, Bob Irwin, who ran the Australia Zoo, cheerfully recalls him as "a monster," and gave Steve a 12-foot scrub python for his 6th birthday. He trapped his first crocodile at the age of 9. While his friend's interactions with animals rarely went beyond opening cans of food for their cats and dogs, Steve was catching fish and hunting rodents to feed his crocodiles and snakes.

Irwin credited his parents with instilling his passion for wildlife. The father and son team proudly boasted that every crocodile in the zoo – approximately 100 in number – was either caught by their bare hands, or bred in the Zoo. On September 4, 2006, Steve's life ended in a tragic, but somehow appropriate way for the man who pioneered Wildlife Warriors Worldwide. While filming an episode for his show, Steve was fatally poisoned by a stingray and died within moments. His death was a loss for the millions who loved him, and for the wild creatures he loved and gave his life to protect.

Steve's enthusiasm for wildlife left little time for lunch, coffee breaks, or small talk at the office water cooler, as long as there was still work to be done.

Evaluate the degree of your enthusiasm for your work. Where does it fall on the following scale?

101-125	It is my delight!
76-100	Count me in
51-75	Maybe there is something to this
26-50	Don't ask me to get involved
0-25	Sorry, I'm not here

POWER TOOLS

*May the God of hope fill you with
all joy and peace as you trust in Him,
so that you may overflow with hope
by the power of the Holy Spirit.*
(Romans 15:13)

*But it is the spirit of man, the
breadth of the Almighty that gives
him understanding.*
(Job 32:8)

*Into your hands, I commit my spirit;
redeem me O Lord, the God of truth.*
(Psalm 31:15)

*God hath raised us up together
and made us sit together in
Heavenly places in Jesus Christ.*
(Ephesians 2:6)

CONSIDER THE TOPIC OF
"Enthusiasm"

ANSWER THE QUESTIONS BELOW TO ENHANCE
YOUR LEADERSHIP SKILLS.

1. How does this characteristic show up in your life?

_____

_____

_____

2. What is it trying to reveal or teach you? What can you learn from it? What awareness does it trigger?

_____

_____

_____

3. How might you use this awareness to make positive changes in your life?

_____

_____

_____

4. Are you willing to live your life differently? In what way?

_____

_____

_____

CHAPTER THREE

Excellent Leadership Results in Excellent Leaders

RANK DOES NOT CONFER PRIVILEGE OR POWER.
IT IMPOSES RESPONSIBILITY.
Peter Drucker

hat is Leadership? According to Webster's dictionary, it is the process of working with and through others to achieve organizational objectives in a changing environment.

If you are a leader, you know that you are challenged each day to improve productivity, decrease costs and run day-to-day operations. You also know that leadership involves influencing people to get the job done.

As the leader, you help create a positive environment in which individuals can be excited, motivated and enthusiastic. Such a positive environment directly affects employees' abilities and desires to produce at their highest potential. Studies, in fact, suggest that the work environment can contribute to at least 20 to 30 percent of business performance.

So if environment drives business performance, what drives the environment? Further studies show that approximately 50 to 70 percent of how employees feel about their organization's environment can be traced to the attitude of one person: the leader.

What a key responsibility that is in an organization! How do you learn the critical skills that will make you a true leader? What turns the novice into the master, capable of motivating and leading others?

According to a study done by Honeywell, leaders learned 50 per cent of what they knew about leading others from on-the-job-assignments. The balance was learned from the "School of Hard Knocks" (20 percent), and from relationships with bosses, mentors and colleagues (30 percent).

Unfortunately, many leaders do not learn these people skills. Although the United States has one of the highest productivity levels in the world, poor leadership seriously affects the quality of life for many workers, both at work and at home.

Leadership styles are very different today. The coercion, fear and threats of punishment that worked ten or twenty years ago are gone. Increasingly, employees want to use their own best judgment.

A Harvard Business Review study found that successful leaders respond to the challenges of their jobs in nontraditional ways.

YOUR ROLE AS A LEADER HAS SHIFTED TO THAT OF COACH SO THAT THE TEAM CAN WIN!

They network, coach, communicate, influence, and mentor while asking questions of the team so they can get positive and negative information.

In order to succeed, leaders must write a new social contract with employees, one that gives them access to more information and greater latitude for decision-making. Your role as a leader has shifted to that of coach so that the team can win!

CASE ILLUSTRATION
Uncommon Business Results

The leadership techniques that helped Carlos Ghosn achieve uncommon business results to bring Nissan Motors back to profitability is detailed in David Magee's book, *Turnaround*. Magee gives us a behind-the-scenes look at Ghosn and tells us that within five days of officially starting at Nissan, Ghosn made the decision to empower the employees. He wanted to preserve the best the culture had to offer within the company, unleashing the talents and ideas he knew were there, through motivation, cultivation, and confidence. He did this through cross-functional teams (CFTs). The company was in debt to the tune of nearly $20 billion dollars in 1999, but as a result of Ghosn's initiatives, Nissan reported a record year in revenues, operating profit, net income, sales volumes and production in 2005 – decidedly the most spectacular reversals in global corporate history. According to Magee, Ghosn knew that leaders must have their own opinions and beliefs in order to lead in a crisis, but in corporate turnarounds – particularly one like Nissan's – protecting the company's identity and the self-esteem of the people was at the forefront.

POWER TOOLS

Whatever is true, whatever is noble,
whatever is right, whatever is pure,
whatever is lovely, whatever is
admirable, if anything is excellent or
praiseworthy, think about such things.
Whatever you have learned or received
or heard from me or seen in me –
put it into practice and the God
of peace will be with you.
(Philippians 4:8-9)

Then, this Daniel was preferred above
the presidents and princes, because an
excellent spirit was in him, and the king
thought to set him over the whole realm.
(Daniel 6:3)

Hear; for I will speak of excellent
things; and the opening of my lips
shall be right things.
(Proverbs 8:6)

CONSIDER THE TOPIC OF
"Excellence"

1. How does this characteristic show up in your life?

_____

_____

_____

2. What is it trying to reveal or teach you? What can you learn from it? What awareness does it trigger?

_____

_____

_____

3. How might you use this awareness to make positive changes in your life?

_____

_____

_____

4. Are you willing to live your life differently? In what way?

_____

_____

_____

CHAPTER FOUR

Simply People

NO MATTER WHAT GREAT THINGS YOU ACCOMPLISH,
SOMEBODY HELPS YOU.
Wilma Rudolph

W)hen you get right down to it, people are the same the world over. We may have a different lot in life, but all of us have the same basic wants and needs.

Psychologist Abraham Maslow proposed that all humans have a hierarchy of needs, and his message holds as true today as when he introduced it in the 1940s. His message was simple: People always have needs. When one need is fulfilled, another emerges in a predictable sequence to take its place. Our needs range from physical survival and safety, to love, public esteem and self-actualization. According to Maslow, most people are not consciously aware of these needs; yet, all people proceed up the same hierarchy of needs, one level at a time.

The rich man and the poor man want and need food. Both women and men want and need love and affection. The president and the company clerk want to be accepted and respected.

One of my jobs was manager of university relations for an automotive company. I was the point person for 35 executives who had recruiting relationships with key colleges and universities. I worked with them to build those relationships, traveling across the country with each of them as they met with university presidents or foundation executives.

Sitting in a limo or corporate jet next to the vice chairman, vice president, or general manager, I was exposed to the way "they" lived. Each trip was different, because each executive was different.

Some trips were uncomfortable. From the conversation and invisible dynamics, the message was that I was in the company of someone who was important. These individuals allowed the status of their position to overshadow their humanness. But, there were others who had a genuine, unpretentious way of dealing with others. These were the people I enjoyed being around.

I recall one trip with a vice president, to an Ivy League university business school where he would be the distinguished lecturer of the evening. We traveled by private jet, just the two of us. During the flight, we chatted about the weather, about business and about the upcoming presentation he would be making. I had arranged part of the itinerary and would assist him on the trip, telling him who would attend the presentation and who he would meet with for private discussions.

When we arrived at the private airport in New Jersey, we were met by a limo and given the full red carpet treatment. Several people from the university – including the dean and associate dean – were among those gathered to greet us. They must have assumed I was his "bag person" rather than a manager, because they totally attempted to ignore me.

What was so special about being in the company of this executive was that he never once allowed me to be ignored by others. He included me in all conversations and at one point indicated to a female executive who was focusing her entire attention on him that if she wanted funding from our company, she was addressing the wrong person. He smiled at me and said, "Lisa is the person responsible for taking your request to the corporation's review board. You'll definitely need to get on her calendar and get to know her."

> ONCE WE REALIZE THAT THERE IS LITTLE DIFFERENCE BETWEEN PEOPLE, WE CAN BEGIN TO TREAT ALL WITH THE SAME POSITIVE REGARD AND RESPECT.

What a relief to be in the company of someone who treated people with dignity and understood that we are all simply people! Because of his dedication, honesty, integrity and attitude of excellence, he continues to excel, inspire others and cultivate a winning organization.

Whether someone has one dime or a million dollars, whether they are in a tuxedo or shabby clothing, and regardless of their gender, age, ethnicity, or beliefs, they deserve respect. The true leader shows respect by interacting with people – socially or professionally – where they are, and accepting them for who they are.

Every day, at home and on the job, we work with people. How we work with them makes a world of difference in the responses we receive. Given the opportunity, people will grow not only in their abilities to perform well at work, but also in their private lives. Once we realize that there is little difference between people, we can begin to treat all with the same positive regard and respect.

CASE ILLUSTRATION
Uncommon Respect

George Madison entered the prestigious hotel's lobby, somewhat shabbily dressed and carrying a large brown paper bag. Based on his appearance, the bellman threatened to call security if he didn't leave at once. Mr. Madison announced that he was checking into the hotel for a weeklong stay, and proceeded to the front desk. The desk clerk refused to acknowledge his presence until Mr. Madison cleared his throat and asked to check in. The clerk, assuming he was a vagabond, quickly stated that there were no rooms available unless he had a reservation.

Mr. Madison – a millionaire – shared his displeasure about the hotel staff's disrespect and lack of courtesy with the manager, and then checked in to a competitor's hotel down the street.

POWER TOOLS

My brothers, as believers in one
glorious Lord, Jesus Christ,
don't show favoritism.
(James 2:1)

Withhold not good from them
to whom it is due, when it is in the
power of thine hand to do it.
(Proverbs 3:27)

A good name is rather to be
chosen than great riches and loving
favor rather than silver and gold.
(Proverbs 22:1)

Be wise in the way you act
towards outsiders.
(Colossians 4:5)

CONSIDER THE TOPIC OF
"Respect"

**ANSWER THE QUESTIONS BELOW TO ENHANCE
YOUR LEADERSHIP SKILLS.**

1. How does this characteristic show up in your life?

_____

_____

_____

2. What is it trying to reveal or teach you? What can you learn from it? What awareness does it trigger?

_____

_____

_____

3. How might you use this awareness to make positive changes in your life?

_____

_____

_____

4. Are you willing to live your life differently? In what way?

_____

_____

_____

CHAPTER FIVE

Pulse Check

I'M LOOKING IN THE MIRROR AND
MAKING ADJUSTMENTS WHERE NEEDED.
Unknown

Without any special training, we are all able to take the measure of people and places. The look a person wears, or the posture they take can tell us more about what is really going on in an organization – the undercurrents and the culture – than a 1,000-page report.

As a leader, you have the power to create an environment in which people can increase their self-esteem while contributing to a greater whole. What a tremendous opportunity!

The first step to achieving this goal is to do a pulse check. What do you see when you observe your employees? A good leader sees how people respond to messages, communications, and assignments; a good leader works to preserve the wellbeing and dignity of everyone involved.

Equally important, what do your employees see when they look at you? Do they see a leader they can believe in? A leader they want to follow? Do the actions you take represent the words you speak? Is your spirit one of compassion, concern and caring?

DO THE ACTIONS YOU TAKE REPRESENT THE WORDS YOU SPEAK?

The interest and excitement you generate as a leader is highly contagious. It is a spirit that activates others and engages the energy of all who experience it. The more you understand yourself and your responsibility as a leader of people, the more engaging you become. Be concerned, be compassionate, and be committed to improving the quality of your life and the people around you. When you are enthused, you can magnetize your employees to the organization's purpose.

To create a setting where people are motivated, excited and enthusiastic about their work, you must become a credible, responsive person. Employees become enthusiastic and get involved when they see a leader who sets a positive example. People have a natural respect for leaders who can be themselves and don't squander their energy putting on performances. Leaders who reveal themselves are far more successful at inspiring others than those who exaggerate themselves and their worth. These leaders are not afraid to do their own thinking, and even more importantly, they are not afraid to engage their employees and empower them to use their knowledge and creativity.

As leaders, we must be concerned with more than personal gain in our own careers. We must be concerned with the impact of our words and deeds, which are much more than what we say or do. The manner in which we deliver our words and deeds reflect who we are.

CASE ILLUSTRATION
Leading by Example

Some of the wealthiest among Nehemiah's people had taken advantage of others by practicing manipulation based on greed and selfishness. Nehemiah displayed extraordinary leadership skills by recognizing the impact his own actions had on people throughout the country. As governor of Judah, he felt that setting a higher standard was his responsibility.

With his position, Nehemiah was granted a special food allowance. For a period of twelve years, he refused to accept it so as not to burden and tax the people.

He was a visionary who inspired others, and was compelled to humbly work alongside everyone else. Nehemiah set priorities and kept them straight when confronted with opposition as well as when he gained success. He set an example for others to follow.

His influence was powerful because he cared about the needs of the people. Instead of being concerned about himself, he was a model that others emulated, and did not take advantage of his position as governor.

In our own time, Henry Ford's great-grandson Bill Ford, Jr., vowed to forego salary, stock and options until the company's automotive operations return to profitability. Likewise, In the 1980s, Lee Iacocca, then-Chairman of Chrysler Corporation, reduced his own salary to $1.00 per

---

year, to show that everyone at the company would have to sacrifice if the company was to survive. Like Nehemiah, these men demonstrated a higher level of leadership – commitment to the good of their organizations and people.

POWER TOOLS

Remember me, my God, for
good, according to all that I have
done for this people.
(Nehemiah 5:19)

Behold, I send you out as sheep
in the midst of wolves. Therefore, be
wise as serpents and harmless as doves.
(Matthew 10:16)

Either make the tree good and
its fruit good, or else make the
tree bad and its fruit bad: for
a tree is know by its fruit.
(Matthew 12:33)

CONSIDER THE TOPIC OF
"Leading By Example"

**ANSWER THE QUESTIONS BELOW TO ENHANCE
YOUR LEADERSHIP SKILLS.**

1. How does this characteristic show up in your life?

_____

_____

_____

2. What is it trying to reveal or teach you? What can you learn from it? What awareness does it trigger?

_____

_____

_____

3. How might you use this awareness to make positive changes in your life?

_____

_____

_____

4. Are you willing to live your life differently? In what way?

_____

_____

_____

CHAPTER SIX

Attitude is a Choice

YOUR LIVING IS DETERMINED NOT SO MUCH BY WHAT
LIFE BRINGS TO YOU AS BY THE ATTITUDE YOU BRING TO LIFE;
NOT SO MUCH BY WHAT HAPPENS TO YOU AS BY THE WAY
YOUR MIND LOOKS AT WHAT HAPPENS.

John Homer Miller

*I*n my career, I've met with people at all organizational levels. I've seen executives who treat employees with respect, and others who think they are the cream in the coffee. The same is true at lower levels in the organization. It's a matter of attitude rather than fact.

ATTITUDES DICTATE OUR RELATIONSHIPS. THEY DETERMINE WHAT WE DO IN OUR RELATIONSHIPS - HOW WE CHOOSE TO THINK AND ACT.

Attitudes dictate our relationships. They determine what we do in our relationships — how we choose to think and act. Frequently, the difference between people who are successful and those who are not is attitude. It's the way they treat others that makes some successful and others not.

Like me, you've probably been around people who consistently say negative things about others. I once worked with a manager who would make statements about people as soon as they left the room, or just before they came in. His remarks were frequently dehumanizing or downright insulting, like the day he said, "Barbara is dumber than a bag of rocks."

In commenting about one of my earlier bosses, he once said, "Sue is like a shark with teeth on both sides of her mouth. She's something, isn't she? She's a survivor." It was a distasteful comment. Even worse, I sensed that he wanted me to say something negative in return, so he could pass that gossip on to someone else.

> IF WE PUT PEOPLE BEFORE THINGS, PEOPLE BEFORE POLICY, PEOPLE BEFORE PROJECTS, WE'RE MAKING A CHOICE.

Remembering how my grandmother handled gossip or idle chatter, I didn't respond to his negative remarks. Instead I said, "I really wouldn't know. I don't make comments like that about people." That stopped him in his tracks, and he never made comments like that to me again.

The attitude we have toward people is of our own choosing. It's our choice to think positively or negatively of others. If we put people before things, people before policy, people before projects, we're making a choice.

A company and its leadership caring for its people is also a matter of choice. A caring company establishes trust with its people, which generates enthusiasm. Wages and perks are not the only things that pay off – employees who are trusted are engaged.

They feel free to be creative and productive. Frequently, they contribute more than what they're paid for. They slide in to home plate head first, each and every time.

We choose our leadership styles. We can choose to be a leader people will follow or one that people will not follow. It is truly a matter of choice to value and appreciate our employees and create an environment that makes them feel worthwhile.

CASE ILLUSTRATION
Attitude is a Choice

After the people of Israel left Egypt and reached the land of Canaan, they were ready to receive their inheritance – the Promised Land – yet their grumbling was the evidence of their disbelief that would keep them from it. They showed no gratitude for God's goodness. Their grumbling had become a contagious habit, an attitude mirroring distrust.

The people thought they should spy out the land before conquering it; God told Moses to send in spies to investigate the land, and twelve spies were chosen. They see that the land is exactly as God said it would be – flowing with milk and honey.

Upon return to their camp, however, they give a divided report – much like any modern day committee. Ten of the spies said, "It flows with milk and honey but there are giants in the land and we are like grasshoppers." The other two spies – Joshua and Caleb – gave a different report, saying, "It truly flows with milk and honey and the people who live there are strong, but we are well able to overcome it."

How quickly, in our lives, we forget what God has done for us! God brought the people of Israel out of Egypt – what could the giants do to them? If God is for us, who can be against us?

The same is true today. We find ourselves grumbling with poor attitudes, not grateful attitudes. If we take the attitude of Joshua and Caleb, we will choose to see the glass half full rather than half empty.

POWER TOOLS

*Whoever has no rule over
his own spirit is like a city
broken down, without walls.*
(Proverbs 25:28)

*Cast away from you all the
transgressions which you have
committed, and get yourselves
a new heart and a new spirit.*
(Ezekiel 18:31)

*Let us choose to use judgment:
let us know among ourselves
what is good.*
(Job 34:4)

CONSIDER THE TOPIC OF
"Positive Attitude"

ANSWER THE QUESTIONS BELOW TO ENHANCE
YOUR LEADERSHIP SKILLS.

1. How does this characteristic show up in your life?

_____

_____

_____

2. What is it trying to reveal or teach you? What can you learn from it? What awareness does it trigger?

_____

_____

_____

3. How might you use this awareness to make positive changes in your life?

_____

_____

_____

4. Are you willing to live your life differently? In what way?

_____

_____

_____

CHAPTER SEVEN

Beyond Business as Usual

YOU CAN OUTDO YOU, IF YOU REALLY WANT TO.
Paul Harvey

"I'll get back with you as soon as we climb to 30,000 feet," said Dave, our pilot. He and his co-pilot had come out of the cockpit to speak to the five passengers on this 12-seater commuter plane. The two were outgoing and friendly as they explained that they expected a bumpy ride.

I was not too pleased to hear about the bumpy ride ahead, but I had to take this trip. I told Dave I was very nervous and that I hoped he'd pilot our flight from Monroe, Louisiana to Memphis Tennessee safely.

He smiled and said, "I pilot a safe operation here, and the more you fly on the small ones the more you'll get the same confidence level that you have on a larger plane."

At 30,000 feet, Dave pulled back the cockpit curtain and asked if I wanted to learn a little more about flying and commuter planes. He put me in the first seat, right behind the cockpit so I could see the instrument panel and look out the front window. He and his co-pilot also provided a set of headphones so I could hear the air traffic controller.

As I listened on the headphones, Dave showed me how the plane operated and how he received information from the air traffic controller. As I learned about the aircraft's operation, I began to feel easier about the trip. When Dave next asked me how I felt, I remarked that I wasn't nervous at all. He'd gone beyond the call of duty to make me feel comfortable.

Then Dave asked me if I was from around the area. I told him that my hometown is Greenville, Mississippi. He said, "You will not believe this! We're flying right over that area in 20 minutes! Is there anyone you want to call and tell that you're flying over their house?" This was long before telephones were available to airplane passengers. I gave him my mother's number. He relayed it to the air traffic controller and called my mother. Was she ever surprised! Was I ever pleased!

The point of this story is that first-rate service doesn't come from a human resource policy handbook, it comes from people who care. As representatives of their company, Dave and his co-pilot went out of their way to ensure that their nervous passenger was completely at ease.

Maintaining a competitive edge in today's fast-paced, ever-changing market place is a challenge. To meet this challenge, we must embrace change, and go beyond "business as usual."

Employees need to feel empowered to contribute to the business.

Consider the history of business. It's filled with stories of outstanding companies and products that disappeared simply because leaders were unwilling to adapt when new circumstances dictated change.

FIRST-RATE SERVICE DOESN'T COME FROM A HUMAN RESOURCE POLICY HANDBOOK, IT COMES FROM PEOPLE WHO CARE

I have visited operations and factories where I felt hope for the future, and left soaring high as a bird in the sky. I have also visited facilities where I felt flat, tired, even bored – and couldn't get excited or enthused about the environment.

The difference is employee enthusiasm and motivation. Employee enthusiasm is linked directly to the spirit of the organization's leadership. For many corporate cultures, creating an enthusiastic work force is highly out of character.

Competition today demands that you get the best from people. To capture the hearts and minds of others, you have to stand back and ask, "What can I do as a leader to insure that people will want to go the extra mile consistently?" You have to think beyond business as usual to earn the enthusiasm and support of others.

What does it mean to go the extra mile? I'll never forget the time I bought my first luxury car. I walked into the dealership and was greeted by salesman Craig Hall. Craig had great enthusiasm for his job. He knew his product, and he was eager to go the extra mile to deliver outstanding customer service. After I decided on the vehicle I wanted to purchase, Craig said to me, "You'll need to drive your old car home, while we prep the new one, and I'll deliver it to you at 9 a.m." I said I'd be at work, and he said, "No problem."

The next morning at 9 a.m. sharp, I received a call from the front desk receptionist stating that a Mr. Craig Hall was waiting in the lobby to see me. When I came out, he asked me if I was ready to take over my new wheels. I followed Craig to the parking lot, and he said, "Hop in on the driver's side." He got in on the passenger side and proceeded to explain how everything on the instrument panel worked. Then he asked me to drive around the block once again to make sure I was satisfied with the operation of my new car.

Just before he left, he said, "I hope you'll enjoy your new car. If you have any problems, concerns, or comments, don't hesitate to call me. And if you ever need your car serviced, always remember there is a loaner at your service. Just call me."

Talk about going beyond the call of duty! I felt very good about my purchase decision and about buying from this particular dealership. Craig's outstanding service made my buying experience memorable. Craig is still in automotive sales today and doing extremely well financially; his enthusiasm and special service keeps customers coming back. Here is what Craig knows: his product is not cars – it is service.

Why does this man convey such enthusiasm? I believe it is because he feels valued by his company and empowered in his job, which translated into a natural outflow of energy, consistency and creativity. Beyond his individual initiative in developing salesmanship skills and professional conduct, it is evident that the dealership encourages and empowers its people to become their best and more.

A sure way to succeed in business is for leadership to go beyond business as usual, which drives the organization to greater heights of achievements.

CASE ILLUSTRATION
It's More than Doing Your Best

W. Edward Deming stood in the front of the lecture theatre and asked, "Do America's Managers understand what must be done?"

Drawn to learn as much as I could from this worldwide renowned voice of quality, I was indeed intrigued by the question and his revolutionary management philosophy.

Working with Dr. Deming as the manager of training for one of he world's largest automotive companies was more than business as usual. In my time with Dr. Deming, I learned that everyone "doing their best" is not enough. They must first know what to do, and follow through with consistency of effort.

Dr. Deming is known for coming up with a set of business principles to help turn around Japan's economy. He did this by asking the country's most influential businessmen to move beyond business as usual. He asked them to improve something about themselves, and something about their product, every day – and to make quality an achievement and a way of life. Within ten years, Japan became an economic world power – by improving one thing each day.

POWER TOOLS

Whatever you do, work at
it with all of your heart,
as working for the Lord,
not for men, since you
know that you will receive an
inheritance from the Lord
as a reward. It is the
Lord Christ you are serving.
(Colossians 3:23-24)

Whatsoever thy
hand findeth to do,
do it with thy might.
(Ecclesiastes 9:10)

Commit your works to the
Lord and your thoughts
will be established.
(Proverbs 16:3)

Do you not know that in a
race all the runners run, but only
one gets the prize? Run in such a
way as to get the prize.
(1Corinthians 9:24)

CONSIDER THE TOPIC OF
"Service and Helpfulness"

ANSWER THE QUESTIONS BELOW TO ENHANCE
YOUR LEADERSHIP SKILLS.

1. How does this characteristic show up in your life?

_____

_____

_____

2. What is it trying to reveal or teach you? What can you learn from it? What awareness does it trigger?

_____

_____

_____

3. How might you use this awareness to make positive changes in your life?

_____

_____

_____

4. Are you willing to live your life differently? In what way?

_____

_____

_____

CHAPTER EIGHT

Why Do You Care?

IF YOU WANT PRODUCTIVITY AND THE FINANCIAL
REWARDS THAT GO WITH IT, YOU MUST TREAT YOUR
WORKERS AS YOUR MOST IMPORTANT ASSET.
Tom Peters

"Why do you care?" he asked. I had been working with Keith for 16 months. When I first arrived at the factory, he said he was tired of teaching management the ropes and never getting anywhere himself. During those first stormy months, he refused to accept the fact that I was his supervisor. He would do what I asked but with a poor attitude. He did not treat me very kindly, and I almost stopped talking to him.

But the spirit inside me refused to let his behavior change my belief in people. About two days before he asked why I cared, we had a conversation about conditions at the factory. I was concerned about the employees because I saw emotional pain on their faces, and had asked him to write down what he saw as morale problems.

Keith filled half a page with examples that showed me leadership was causing undue stress in the workplace, dampening enthusiasm. Clearly, Keith felt frustrated. He would complete an assignment and then find that his work was overturned based upon someone else's needs.

After reading his concerns, I went into his office and told him how much I appreciated his opening up to me. I gave him the following poem as recited by Nelson Mandela and asked him to read it because it reminded me so much of his situation:

Our deepest fear is not that we are inadequate.
Our deepest fear is that we are powerful beyond measure.
It is our light, not our darkness that most frightens us.
We ask ourselves, who am I to be brilliant,
gorgeous, talented and fabulous?
Actually, who are you not to be?
You are a child of God.
Your playing small doesn't serve the world.
There's nothing enlightened about shrinking so
that other people won't feel insecure around you.
We were born to make manifest the glory
of God that is within us.
It's not just in some of us, it's in everyone.
And as we let our own light shine,
we unconsciously give other people
permission to do the same.
As we are liberated from our own fear,
our presence automatically liberates others.

Ten minutes later Keith was standing over my desk, asking me why I cared. "Because I do," I told him. "Because I think you're special, and if I can help you in some small way, let me."

He smiled and seemed to soften. He said, "The poem says a lot about me." We talked, and I asked him to consider how he could lose the chains that bound him. I acknowledged that leadership plays a part in how we feel at work, but I also pointed out that we, too, are responsible for making ourselves feel good.

Keith's response gave me a lot to think about. I reasoned that his reactions to me were really reactions to himself. I had reached out to him with kindness — the simple, basic kindness that people the world over want to receive from others — and he responded positively. His response taught me that I can be the difference in someone's life.

THE POWER OF CARING CAN POSITIVELY INFLUENCE THE LIVES YOU TOUCH.

People respond to kindness. When you show interest and concern and caring for others, they will show interest and concern for you. It's a cause and effect process. Stressing the dignity of the individual will change workers' attitudes and improve their performance. Ultimately, your emphasis on the dignity of the individual will improve and strengthen the entire organization. The power of caring can positively influence the lives you touch.

There is much to learn from employees, but leadership has to be willing to listen. When we give employees an opportunity to get involved, or even the freedom to fail from time to time, we give them the opportunity to commit to the organization and its vision. Employees want to know that they make a difference and that leadership cares. The payoff is rewarding for the employee and the organization.

CASE ILLUSTRATION

The King and His Three Sons — A Fairy Tale of Unknown Origin

Once there was a king, in a faraway land, who gave specific responsibilities to his three sons. The first son was in charge of agriculture and growing food to feed the people. The second son was responsible for the health of the people, and the third son's job was singing and dancing, to keep the spirit of the people uplifted.

The king was called away on a long journey, and entrusted the welfare of his kingdom to his sons. But famine scourged the land, and although the son in charge of agriculture did everything he knew to do, the famine was relentless and took a great toll on the land and the people.

The son responsible for health did all that he could, too – but the people were hungry, and without nourishment, many were seriously ill or lost.

The king returned in the midst of the strife. He saw his barren, devastated fields, and with a saddened heart, called his three sons together to discuss what had happened in his absence.

The first son said he had tried everything, but the famine was so severe, he couldn't grow food for the people, and many of them starved. The king wept, for he understood.

He asked the second son, "Did you minister to the

people?" The son said he had worked many long hours without rest to save the people, but still, many were lost. The king moaned, with a heavy heart, and said that he understood.

He turned to the third son and asked, "Son, did you dance for the people?" The third son quickly replied, "Oh, no! I saw how severe the famine was, and how downtrodden the people were. This was no time to dance and sing or show joy! It would not have been appropriate!"

The king threw his arms around his son and exclaimed, "Oh, my son! This is when people needed your song and dance the most, to lift them above the pain and misery of the conditions, to inspire them and give them hope. When things seem the worst, we need to change our perspective and move from despair to joy."

And so, the third son and his brothers went among the people, singing and dancing. Peace and hope was restored to the kingdom, and the people began to thrive once again.

POWER TOOLS

*Praise be to the God and
Father of our Lord Jesus Christ,
the Father of compassion and the
God of all comfort, who comforts
us in all our troubles, so that we
can comfort those in any trouble
with the comfort we ourselves have
received from God. For just as the
suffering of Christ flows over into
our lives, so also through Christ
our comfort overflows.*
(2 Corinthians 1:3-5)

*Silver or gold I do not have,
but what I have I give you.*
(Acts 3:6)

*And I will pray the Father,
and He will give you another
Helper, that He may abide
with you forever.*
(John 14:16)

CONSIDER THE TOPIC OF
"Caring for Others"

ANSWER THE QUESTIONS BELOW TO ENHANCE
YOUR LEADERSHIP SKILLS.

1. How does this characteristic show up in your life?

_____

_____

_____

2. What is it trying to reveal or teach you? What can you learn from it? What awareness does it trigger?

_____

_____

_____

3. How might you use this awareness to make positive changes in your life?

_____

_____

_____

4. Are you willing to live your life differently? In what way?

_____

_____

_____

Chapter Nine

Communication: The First Principle of Life

HE CREATED US AS A PART OF THE DIVINE PLAN
FOR FELLOWSHIP WITH HIM AND OTHERS.
Genesis, Chapter 1

Given today's organizational culture in which team-work is crucial to getting things done, good communication is more important than ever before, and requires skill in many forms. We communicate face-to-face, by telephone, email, and text messaging. We have conversations, and make presentations. We send e-mail and deliver reports. We use words and body language.

As human beings, communication is an essential part of our being. We have a deep need for relating to others, and the quality of our communication is frequently the make-or-break issue in any team — be it a marriage, child-parent relationship or work group. You may have noticed that often the best times we have are when we're talking with friends or colleagues and the communication channels are clear. Everything flows, and we feel wonderful. In any arena, mastering how we communicate is key to being successful.

One of the biggest challenges leaders face is motivating employees to understand and voluntarily work toward the organization's objectives. Effective communication is key because it drives cooperation, which drives trust. It connects by getting everyone moving in the same direction. Psychological research suggests that relationships built on trust are *predictable, caring, and faithful.* When, over time, a manager's behavior is consistent and employees are able to count on that behavior, it builds trust. By contrast, it is difficult to trust anyone – employer or employee – whose actions are inconsistent or unpredictable.

EFFECTIVE COMMUNICATION IS THE KEY BECAUSE IT DRIVES COOPERATION WHICH DRIVES TRUST.

That you may spend the majority of your time communicating verbally or in written form doesn't mean your communications are effective.

How can you improve your ability to communicate effectively? By understanding that communication is not just verbal, and it is not something that happens just when we're talking. Constantly, in everything we do, we are communicating, sending out messages that others pick up on and hear. Communication has to do with the climate we create, the climate in which employees work.

Make sure you understand your audience and your message. Be clear about what you're trying to accomplish.

Here are six ways to improve your communications on a daily basis:

1. *Walk your talk.* Talk is cheap. When you practice what you preach and actually do what you say you're going to do, you gain the respect and trust of others.

2. *Be upbeat.* You are an ambassador for your company or organization. If you are excited and enthused, others will follow your example.

3. *Give the big picture.* Consistently communicate the core message of what the company or organization is about to your employees. Share the task at hand and also the vision and goals with all of your employees, not just some of them. When employees feel they are active participants in change, they are more likely to get enthused and involved.

4. *Be sincere and straightforward.* Don't try to impress people with fancy words and long speeches. The idea is to get your message across, so be concise and specific.

5. *Be respectful and courteous of others' feelings.* Whispering in meetings or in the company of others excludes people and makes them feel uncomfortable, even if you're not talking about them. If you need to speak with someone privately, wait for an appropriate time when you won't need to whisper or move to a different location, if possible.

6. *Listen to others.* Don't attempt to know everything. If you listen, you might hear and learn something new.

CASE ILLUSTRATION
Communications/Trust Model

In the film *Survival Run* by Pyramid Media, marathon runner Harry Cordello runs the difficult Dipsea course, an annual event through the majestic mountains, deep ravines and lush forests of Marin County, California. Harry, who is blind, is guided through the course by the voice, and the occasional nudge of the arm, of his sighted partner, Mike Restani. This film is used in many training courses as an unforgettable study of a highly motivated team that overcomes seemingly insurmountable limitations to achieve a goal. Because Harry is blind, he must trust Mike to make critical decisions, guide him through the challenging course, and lead him to the finish line. His race, and his success as a runner, is in Mike's hands. To build this level of trust, Harry and his friend experienced the elements of a Communications/Trust Model, which says that in order to have trust two things must occur.

The first is bottom line communications. Harry was able to run the course because his friend provided precise instructions and details of the terrain ahead. Mike spoke; Harry listened and responded in the knowledge that Mike's words were true.

The second is cooperation. In order for Harry to run the marathon, he needed Mike's cooperation – he needed to be willing to make Mike his "team leader," and have faith that Mike would follow through on his commitment to guide him through the course. At the same time, Mike needed to know that Harry would follow his guidance and stay the course with him. Trust was obviously at the foundation of their relationship, and was clearly a compelling force as Mike skillfully led Harry through the difficult Dipsea course.

THE COMMUNICATION/TRUST MODEL:

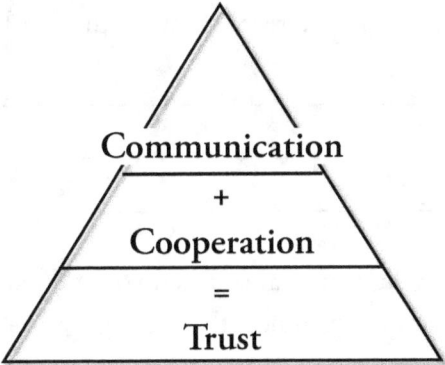

CONSIDER THE TOPIC OF
"Effective Communication"

ANSWER THE QUESTIONS BELOW TO ENHANCE
YOUR LEADERSHIP SKILLS.

1. How does this characteristic show up in your life?

_____

_____

_____

2. What is it trying to reveal or teach you? What can you learn from it? What awareness does it trigger?

_____

_____

_____

3. How might you use this awareness to make positive changes in your life?

_____

_____

_____

4. Are you willing to live your life differently? In what way?

_____

_____

_____

POWER TOOLS

Hear; for I will speak of excellent
things; and the opening of my
lips shall be right things.
(Proverbs 8:6)

The tongue of the wise useth knowledge
aright; but the mouth
of fools poured out foolishness.
(Proverbs 15:2)

Only let your conversation be as
it becometh the gospel of Christ.
(Philippians 1:27)

A man hath joy by the answer
of his mouth; and a word spoken in
due season, how good it is!
(Proverbs 15:23)

CHAPTER TEN

The Art of Listening

LISTENING IS AN ART; NO CONVERSATION
SHOULD BE WITHOUT IT.
John Gardner Jr.

hen my son was sixteen and forming his own opinions and judgments, he told me how he viewed me. I have to say it caught me off guard. I heard him, but at the same time I didn't really want to hear what he had to say to me.

The main thing was that he felt I didn't listen to him. I thought about what he said for a few days, then initiated a new discussion.

Attending to our children's words and thoughts and feeling is in our own best interest. As parents, we have to help our kids achieve their best, in every way possible. A key ingredient to their winning is giving them the best that we have to offer. That means listening to them.

The same applies in the workplace. This is not unlike the employer/employee relationship. Employees tell us, in many different ways, how we are viewed and how we are doing, but typically we don't choose to hear them.

Being a good listener is crucial for good communication. To get full involvement means we must give full attention. If employees don't receive the benefit of our time and attention, we lose them. Our employees will go through the motions – they'll check in and check out every day – but we will have lost everything they have to offer. To have enthusiasm and to inspire enthusiasm from others, we need to listen and hear.

TO HAVE ENTHUSIASM AND TO INSPIRE ENTHUSIASM FROM OTHERS, WE NEED TO LISTEN AND HEAR.

Do we fully understand what the other person is saying?

To get the most from a conversation, turn your attention to the person talking. Put yourself in that person's shoes. Rather than letting yourself be distracted by other things, listen attentively. When you do, you tell people they are important and that they are worth your time and attention. We all have been around leaders who feel they are too important to listen to us. How irritating and frustrating! Most of us gain immensely by listening to people from all walks of life. Whether employee, friend, colleague, child, boss or client, the diversity of people in this world offers wealth, if only we open ourselves to receive it.

CASE ILLUSTRATION
Should I Repeat that?

" Hi, may I come in to speak with you for a moment? I have a lot on my mind and would like your opinion."

"Sure, have a seat," the supervisor said, although he didn't turn around to acknowledge Ted until after he sat down.

"What's on your mind?"

Before Ted had completed his first sentence, the supervisor jumped in with a comment, and continued to interrupt throughout the meeting. He was impatient, repeatedly finished Ted's sentences for him, and answered several phone calls. His impatience, interruptions and assumptions about what Ted had to say caused a "disconnect" for Ted.

Do you truly listen to your employees and let them finish their thoughts? Effective listening is a powerful art that can generate great returns for the positive mood of an organization, and you as a leader. People respect and gravitate to great listeners because they feel acknowledged.

POWER TOOLS

*Let your conversation be
always full of grace, seasoned
with salt so you will know
how to answer everyone.*
(Colossians 4:6)

*Wherefore, my beloved brethren,
let every man be swift to hear,
slow to speak, slow to wrath.*
(James 1:19)

*He that hath an ear, let
him hear what the spirit
sayeth unto the churches.*
(Revelation 2:7)

*Listen, my son, to
your father's instruction
and do not forsake your
mother's teaching.*
(Proverbs 1:8)

CONSIDER THE TOPIC OF
"Effective Listening"

ANSWER THE QUESTIONS BELOW TO ENHANCE
YOUR LEADERSHIP SKILLS.

1. How does this characteristic show up in your life?

_____

_____

_____

2. What is it trying to reveal or teach you? What can you learn from it? What awareness does it trigger?

_____

_____

_____

3. How might you use this awareness to make positive changes in your life?

_____

_____

_____

4. Are you willing to live your life differently? In what way?

_____

_____

_____

CHAPTER ELEVEN

Positive / Negative Exchanges

LIFE IS THE MIRROR OF EVERYONE. IN JUST WHAT YOU
SAY AND DO, GIVE TO THE WORLD THE BEST YOU HAVE
AND THE BEST WILL COME BACK TO YOU.
J. C. Gardner, Sr.

Interpersonal relationships have a profound effect in shaping our daily lives. Our interactions with others — children, spouses, friends, co-workers, or supervisors — are a basic element of our lives. How we treat others is representative of how we expect to be treated. As the old saying goes, "What goes around comes around." This truth is fundamental in shaping our environments.

OUR INTERACTIONS WITH OTHERS — ARE A BASIC ELEMENT OF OUR LIVES.

If you practice the exchange principle of life, you will get what you give. Treat people kindly, and you will get kindness in return. Once you decide to make positive exchange a daily practice in your relationships, you will grow professionally and spiritually.

My grandfather worked for 53 years as an insurance agent for Universal Life Insurance Company. He received a community service award at the age of 86 when he retired.

He was a tall, thin, statuesque man, and as a little girl I loved to walk with him on his rounds to collect insurance premiums. The hat, the suit, the white shirt, the tie, the shined shoes, the briefcase under his arm, the long stride of his legs, the gentle waving of his hands — everything about him made me feel safe and proud to be with him.

We had a game I never tired of playing. For every one step or stride he took, I'd have to take three. How I loved keeping up with him, so that I could get the twenty-five cents he promised! That was my grandfather's way of teaching me to walk at a steady pace with a goal in mind.

More importantly, as we passed along the neighborhood houses, I remember hearing and seeing the smiles and greetings from all who knew him. "Hello, Mr. Gardner, how are you today? Mr. Gardner, it's so good to see you." Some people would even come out to shake his hand. I felt so proud just being next to him and being able to call him my granddaddy.

What I learned from associating with my grandfather was that he had a winning spirit, displayed daily in the way he dressed and carried himself, and the manner in which he treated people. Though he never owned a car, people all over the city knew him and respected him as a high contributor to the community.

What I learned most from my grandfather was that for every action in life there is a reaction. The reaction he received was positive because he gave positively and freely.

Although my grandfather didn't have a college education, he stretched my siblings and me by his mere presence, and by his exchanges with us. The wisdom and parables he shared prepared us for hardwork. He gave us a sense of possibility far beyond our existence in the segregated Mississippi Delta. His spirit of kindness, gentleness and firmness was deeply instilled in us, so that we would treat others as we wanted to be treated. Never once did I hear him raise his voice in anger, even when the situation warranted it. His presence alone was enough to let us kids know what his message meant. Yet his attitude was always positive and loving, and in return we were positive and loving with him.

FOR EVERY ACTION IN LIFE THERE IS A REACTION.

The world needs more people like J.C. Gardner — those whose ambitions are large enough to include others...who know that walking over others is not the key to success...who are not afraid to stand up for what they believe in, even in the face of general opinion...who provide good examples which prompt others to follow...who are honest, have integrity and understand that before you can receive you must first be a genuine giver.

CASE ILLUSTRATION
Every Good Work Shows Character

If you observe, for a period of time, two people – one whose days are filled with negative words, places and people, and the other whose days are filled with positive words, places and people – eventually you will notice a distinct difference in the outcome of victories in their lives.

Leaders come in different sizes, shapes, and attitudes. People are usually impressed by the way a person looks, but true leadership comes from what lives inside a person's heart.

David, a great leader in the Old Testament, gives us an excellent model to follow. David exemplified a winning spirit of positive exchanges. Part of his success is based on the personal example he gave as a warrior in battle. The story for which he is best known is his battle with Goliath, and his ability to be unshaken.

Eventually, his strong leadership attracted the very best men of the nation. His personality positively influenced others. This young shepherd with no formal training was able to garner the Israelite army to victory.

Throughout the Bible we learn that David possessed traits of fairness, integrity, respect for others, and humility – even while showing us that he was far from perfect. David shows us that leadership is a matter of character, a winning spirit.

POWER TOOLS

*Remind them to be subject to rulers
and authorities, to obey, to be ready
for every good work, to speak evil of
no one, to be peaceable, gentle,
showing all humility to all men.*
(Titus 3:1)

*A good name is rather to be
chosen than great riches, loving favor
rather than silver and gold.*
(Proverbs 22:1)

*Moreover you shall select from
all the people able men, such as fear
God, men of truth, hating coveteousness;
and place such over them to be rulers
of thousands, rulers of hundred,
rulers of fifties, and rulers of tens.*
(Exodus 18:21)

*Whatever you do, work at it
with all of your heart, as working
for the Lord, not for men.*
(Colossians 3:23)

CONSIDER THE TOPIC OF
"Positive Exchanges"

**ANSWER THE QUESTIONS BELOW TO ENHANCE
YOUR LEADERSHIP SKILLS.**

1. How does this characteristic show up in your life?

_____

_____

_____

2. What is it trying to reveal or teach you? What can you learn from it? What awareness does it trigger?

_____

_____

_____

3. How might you use this awareness to make positive changes in your life?

_____

_____

_____

4. Are you willing to live your life differently? In what way?

_____

_____

_____

Chapter Twelve

Balance the Weight

A FALSE BALANCE IS AN ABOMINATION TO THE LORD;
BUT A JUST WEIGHT IS HIS DELIGHT.
Proverbs 11:1

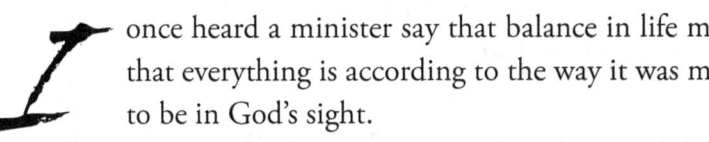 once heard a minister say that balance in life means that everything is according to the way it was meant to be in God's sight.

When employees spend 12-13 hours a day, six or seven days a week on a job, it certainly skews their personal lives, and throws things out of rhythm. When co-workers and bosses are overworked, people unexpectedly blow off steam.

Our personal lives become chaotic when we spend too much time at work and not enough time at home with our families. We become irritable. We stop going to church. We don't spend time with friends, and we stop doing the things we love because we are overloaded. Marriages suffer. Children become unmanageable.

When the scales are unbalanced, something must change. To have balance, we must choose to create it by minimizing stress and overwork.

While each of us is responsible for juggling the demands of work and family life, organizations play a significant role in the balancing act. Too often, leaders who vocalize their support for the balance of work and family don't put these values into practice. They say one thing and do another.

As leaders, we must get past the hypocrisy and walk the talk. There's nothing wrong with enjoyment! Sometimes the corporate culture can put the pressure on and make working hard seem better than working smart.

As a leader, if you truly believe in balance, take these eight steps to ensure that your company supports employee efforts to juggle family and work:

1. Encourage vacations and discourage workaholism.

2. Provide balance seminars as part of development training.

3. Limit business travel on weekends.

4. Limit after-hours meetings.

5. Provide options for employees to include the family at specific work related events.

6. Include balance as a core value of the organization.

7. Discourage bringing work home.

8. Include on-site childcare where possible.

Take the time to take care of yourself and help your employees; remove the organizational and cultural barriers that keep them from achieving balance in their lives. When we can strike a good balance between work and play, life is sweet. All the pieces of the puzzle — work, family, spiritual and personal lives — fit together. Relationships at work and at home improve. We have more energy and enthusiasm, and we feel better emotionally and spiritually. These rewards stir our souls and enhance our ability to accomplish our goals.

WHEN WE CAN STRIKE A GOOD BALANCE BETWEEN WORK AND PLAY, LIFE IS SWEET.

CASE ILLUSTRATION
What are You Doing with Your Time?

To be a good leader, we must live a balanced life. Consider the story of Lazarus, who along with his sisters Mary and Martha, was a close personal friend of Jesus.

Lazarus became ill. Mary and Martha sent for Jesus, to come heal their brother. Even after he received the news, Jesus remained where he was for an additional two days (John 11:6). Martha was disappointed, and surely not pleased with Jesus when, upon his arrival in Judea, she said, "Lord, if thou hads't been here my brother would not have died" (John 11:21).

Jesus shows us that even the emergencies and priorities of others should not keep us off balance. We are daily making choices about the way we spend our time. We are also living with the consequences of our choices. Carefully balancing our lives will give us a greater chance for spending time on what we feel is important in our lives.

While Jesus, on his time and schedule, raised Lazarus from the dead, He provided us a map by which to model our lives. Jesus showed that scales measure the weight on both sides – they are either in balanced, or not. We can add or subtract weights until the sides are equal – until our lives are in harmony. Maintaining a balanced life is God's plan for our lives.

POWER TOOLS

To every thing there is a season,
and a time to every purpose under
the heaven: a time to be born, and
a time to die; a time to plant, and a
time to pluck up that which is planted.
(Ecclesiastics 3:1-2)

Walk in wisdom toward them that
are without, redeeming the time.
(Colossians 4:5)

Honest weights and scales
belong to the Lord; all the weights
in the bag are His work.
(Proverbs 16:11)

CONSIDER THE TOPIC OF
"Balance at Work and Home"

ANSWER THE QUESTIONS BELOW TO ENHANCE
YOUR LEADERSHIP SKILLS.

1. How does this characteristic show up in your life?

_____

_____

_____

2. What is it trying to reveal or teach you? What can you learn from it? What awareness does it trigger?

_____

_____

_____

3. How might you use this awareness to make positive changes in your life?

_____

_____

_____

4. Are you willing to live your life differently? In what way?

_____

_____

_____

CHAPTER THIRTEEN
Recognition Matters

BE A STAR CATCHER. REGULARLY "CATCH PEOPLE DOING
THINGS RIGHT" AND RECOGNIZE THEM FOR IT.
Eric Harvey and Alexander Lucia

*I*t's a moment I'll always remember. So unexpected, so simple, yet it had a lasting influence upon me.

One morning the divisional general manager came to my office, saying, "I just wanted to stop by to say thank you for developing and facilitating a great leadership training conference last week. I think we have some outstanding new supervisors, and they received a jump-start in the right direction. Thanks for your efforts to make it such a successful week of learning." Then he wrote something on a small orange plastic basketball and presented it to me.

I didn't understand why he was giving me a toy-like basketball, but when I read what he'd written, I understood. "Thanks for the assist – Jerry Collins." He told me that sometimes it's easier to make the shots in the basket than to assist the player who makes the shots, and he said, "You've done an outstanding job in assisting our new leaders make good shots. Keep up the good work."

Even today, more than ten years after the fact, I remember his words vividly and the impact they had on my thinking: You don't have to be the star; helping others will bring about recognition and appreciation as well. An assist is as good as a goal.

Truly, Jerry Collins is one of those leaders you remember with a smile, whose example you desire to follow. Giving due recognition builds the fires of enthusiasm and helps to create a supportive work environment in which employees are motivated to get involved and be successful. Leaders who take the time to appreciate their employees serve their organization well and boost productivity.

GIVING DUE RECOGNITION BUILDS THE FIRES OF ENTHUSIASM

Recognition does not always have to take the form of money. Often it's simply a matter of being thoughtful and taking the time to express thanks. Just the simple act of recognizing individuals for their efforts can have a profound effect.

Here are five ways to show appreciation that cost little but have large impact:

1. Sit down one-on-one with the person to say thanks for a job well done.

2. Send a voice mail or e-mail, praising him or her for efforts made.

3. Leave a thank-you card on the individual's desk before he or she arrives to work.

4. Declare an appreciation day for teams or for a number of people who truly deserve recognition.

5. Hand out a blue ribbon that says "Good job; keep up the good work."

People are the lifeblood of an organization. Leaders must reaffirm this truth on a daily basis. Individual employees need to know that they are valued.

CASE ILLUSTRATION
An Assist is as Good as a Goal

An individual's winning streak is expanded if recognition is authentic, honestly aligned with the facts.

There once was a father whose child had difficulty with ordinary things. One winter day, after a heavy snowfall, the father took his son outside to help him clear the snow. The father worked on the long, wide driveway, telling his son to clear the walkway to the front door.

Several hours passed before the father finished clearing the heavy snow from the driveway. Exhausted, he looked up to see his son, slowly clearing the last bits of snow from the walkway.

"Wow, son! That's the cleanest this walkway has ever been in the winter! You've done a great job!" he said. "And I appreciate your help."

The boy beamed and stood a bit taller as he internalized a new and positive attitude about himself. From that day forward, he maintained a winning attitude.

POWER TOOLS

If anyone gives even a cup of cold water
to one of these little ones because
he is my disciple, I tell you the truth,
he will certainly not lose his reward.
(Matthew 10:42)

I the Lord search the heart
and examine the mind, to reward a
man according to his conduct, according
to what his deeds deserve.
(Jeremiah 7:10)

Rejoice and be glad, because
great is your reward in heaven.
(Matthew 5:12)

CONSIDER THE TOPIC OF
"Recognition"

ANSWER THE QUESTIONS BELOW TO ENHANCE
YOUR LEADERSHIP SKILLS.

1. How does this characteristic show up in your life?

_____

_____

_____

2. What is it trying to reveal or teach you? What can you learn from it? What awareness does it trigger?

_____

_____

_____

3. How might you use this awareness to make positive changes in your life?

_____

_____

_____

4. Are you willing to live your life differently? In what way?

_____

_____

_____

CHAPTER FOURTEEN
To Tell the Truth

THE TROUBLE WITH STRETCHING THE TRUTH IS
THAT IT'S APT TO SNAP BACK.
Honor Works

y son and I were standing in the University of Michigan's Chrisler Arena, where boys from across the United States had gathered for the Annual Summer Basketball Camp. Between trying to find a parking space in the parking lot, to standing in various lines to register my son for camp, I could have felt totally frustrated and irritated.

But as we patiently waited in the lines, I noticed that all the helpers at the registration tables were young college students. We were in line to pay a deposit for the dormitory room my son would need during his stay on campus. I gave the young man at the desk $20 for the key deposit. He handed me $10 change and gave my son the key. While he was serving us, he was also talking to a friend nearby. Because he wasn't paying attention, he gave me another $10 as we turned to leave, forgetting he had already given me my change.

I said to him, "Oh, you've already paid me. This $10 does not belong to me." He said, "Oh, yeah, thanks. I forgot I already gave it to you." I said, "Yes, you did."

INTEGRITY MEANS BEING HONEST IN LITTLE SITUATIONS, AS WELL AS BIG ONES.

My son looked at me and said, "Mom, most people wouldn't have done that." I told him, "A person's true character is revealed by their actions — what he or she does when others are watching, and most importantly, when people aren't watching."

Integrity means being honest in little situations as well as big ones. It means living what you say. Integrity and honesty will get you farther than a four-year degree and will grow an organization quicker than self-serving efforts.

In our day-to-day activities at work, we run into people who are honest and those who aren't. What's important for most of us is that we work for an organization that has integrity. Working in an environment that is anything less can be demoralizing.

Integrity should be your foundation. As a leader, do what you say you're going to do. Be considerate of others, and maintain the highest standard of behavior. The tone you set will influence your employees and your children, who will behave in like manner.

CASE ILLUSTRATION
Truth: A Means to Victory

Mahatma Gandhi was certain that the world rested upon the bedrock of truth and untruth, and made truth his strength.

In South Africa, Gandhi fought racial discrimination in a non-violent, purposeful and truthful manner so apparent that his enemies recognized his truth and inner strength. Truth was the end, and non-violence the means, by which Gandhi challenged the social order of South Africa, and later, of India.

Gandhi fought for the cause of the degraded. He believed that the world could be purged of evil by overcoming anger with love, untruth with truth.

Since his death, generations have come to know his work in South Africa and India, because of his unwavering leadership and spiritual courage with truth as the only means to victory.

POWER TOOLS

*For I was very glad when brethren
came and testified to your truth, that is,
how you are walking in truth. I have no
greater joy than this, to hear of my
children walking in truth.*
(3 John 3-4, NASB)

*I am the way, the truth, and
the life: no man cometh unto the
Father, but by Me.*
(John 14:6)

*When the spirit of truth has come,
He will guide you into all truth for
He will not speak on His own authority;
but whatever he hears he will speak
and He will tell you things to come.*
(John 16:13)

*The integrity of the upright
will guide them, but the perversity
of the unfaithful will destroy them.*
(Proverbs 11:3)

CONSIDER THE TOPIC OF
"Truthfulness"

ANSWER THE QUESTIONS BELOW TO ENHANCE
YOUR LEADERSHIP SKILLS.

1. How does this characteristic show up in your life?

_____

_____

_____

2. What is it trying to reveal or teach you? What can you learn from it? What awareness does it trigger?

_____

_____

_____

3. How might you use this awareness to make positive changes in your life?

_____

_____

_____

4. Are you willing to live your life differently? In what way?

_____

_____

_____

CHAPTER FIFTEEN

Who Do You Trust?

HOLD YOURSELF RESPONSIBLE FOR A HIGHER
STANDARD THAN ANYBODY ELSE EXPECTS OF YOU.
Henry Ward Beecher

*M*utual trust doesn't just happen. It is the result of setting aside envy, suspicion, pride, personal agendas, doubt and dishonesty.

I remember as a child a promise made to me by an adult friend about going to the state fair. I expected that promise to be fulfilled, and it wasn't. I was disappointed, and I stopped trusting that friend.

Children look to adults—parents, teachers, family friends— to teach them about honesty, and are confused when they are let down. They think the adult is lying. While a little lie may seem insignificant to the adult, it's much bigger for the child. If a parent tells their child to say they are not home if someone calls on the phone, what does that tell the child about honesty and trust?

There is really no difference between a big lie and a little lie. Dishonesty is dishonesty. "Little white lies" are still lies. Most people believe they are honest and basically good. Oddly enough, many also believe there is nothing wrong with being "a little bit" dishonest. The reality is that, much like water trickling downhill, "a little bit" of dishonesty eventually causes significant erosion in our relationships.

PEOPLE WATCH THE PERSON IN CHARGE TO GAUGE THE CLIMATE AND CHARACTER OF THE REST OF THE ORGANIZATION

As parents, children, teachers, students, employers and employees, we must build our relationships around being trustworthy. Just as parents have to build mutual truth with their kids, leaders must develop mutual trust with employees if the relationship is going to be worthwhile and productive.

Developing mutual trust may entail getting knocked down occasionally by people who violate the trust you place in them. Nonetheless, developing a trusting relationship with others leads to positive outcomes.

When it comes to leadership, people watch the person in charge to gauge the climate and character of the rest of the organization. Your employees expect you to acknowledge when you make a mistake to communicate clearly, without exaggerating or distorting information. Your customers, and those in your community, will not trust your organization if they see that you as a leader cannot be trusted to do what you say.

CASE ILLUSTRATION
Compromise Corrupts Hearts

The truth is not negotiable. What you say is either true or false. Today, our world accepts things as relative – to the level that there are differing degrees of truth.

Since it's collapse in late 2001, Enron Corporation no longer occupies the shiny office tower in Houston. At one point, Enron employed 32,000 workers around the globe, was ranked as the seventh largest public company in America, and was led by executives who made millions of dollars. Today, after the discovery of fraudulent activity and lies, all that is left is a lot of debt and untold numbers of ruined lives.

God wants you to realize that He is the truth and the light, that His word is trustworthy no matter what condition the world is in, or the circumstances you may face. Trusting Him in all situations allows you the freedom to release anxiety, worry, and defeat. Trusting Him without relying on your own strength or the opinions of others will cause others to trust you.

POWER TOOLS

Blessed is the man who trusts in the Lord,
whose confidence is in Him.
(Jeremiah 17:7)

We have renounced the things
hidden because of shame, not walking in
craftiness nor handling the word of God
deceitfully, but by manifestation
of the truth commending ourselves to every
man's conscience in the sight of God.
(2 Corinthians 4)

A fortune made by a lying tongue is a
fleeting vapor and a deadly snare.
(Proverbs 21:6)

Trust in the Lord with all thine
heart; and lean not unto thine own
understanding. In all thy ways acknowledge
Him, and He shall direct thy path.
(Proverbs 3:5-6)

CONSIDER THE TOPIC OF
"Trust"

1. How does this characteristic show up in your life?

_____

_____

_____

2. What is it trying to reveal or teach you? What can you learn from it? What awareness does it trigger?

_____

_____

_____

3. How might you use this awareness to make positive changes in your life?

_____

_____

_____

4. Are you willing to live your life differently? In what way?

_____

_____

_____

CHAPTER SIXTEEN
Creativity Power

TRY OUT YOUR IDEAS BY
VISUALIZING THEM IN ACTION.
David Seabury

Successful companies encourage people to blaze new trails and take meaningful risks at a reasonable cost. The "American Family" culture within Southwest Airlines puts it at the top of the list of desired employers; Harley-Davidson has built a cult status with their customers, employees and investors over the one hundred and three year history of the company, despite intense competition from overseas. Add Levi Strauss and Microsoft to the list – they've all achieved significant returns on the investments they've made in their people.

Sadly, most organizations do little to encourage the creativity they claim to want. Typically, the employees who are willing to take risks and innovate are seen as outcasts or simply not part of the team. The " good old boy network" sends the message that

COMPANIES THAT ENCOURAGE PEOPLE TO BLAZE NEW TRAILS AND TAKE MEANINGFUL RISKS AT A REASONABLE COST ARE THOSE THAT SUCCEED.

it is not okay to be creative or different unless you are part of the group.

Leaders who recognize and encourage creativity are rewarded with the best achievements of their employees. Creative employees are enthusiastic workers because the thought of being valuable gives meaning to their work. They stretch themselves and take the organization to new levels of achievement. Creativity should be linked to individual employee performance measurement and feedback goals. It should be an integral part of the work ethic, and valued as such.

Encouraging creativity in your organization is a powerful tool. Albert Einstein said, "Imagination is more important than knowledge. Knowledge is limited. Imagination encircles the world." Imagination created the universe. Everything – every idea, every concept, every tool, every relationship – began as thoughts. When motivational speakers and preachers say, "You can't see what you haven't conceived," they speak the truth.

We form a desire in our hearts. The desire becomes a vision, the vision is translated into words. It is only when we turn the vision and the words into action that we truly create.

We are creative beings. It is this creativity that gives us joy and satisfaction. Just as God created the world and pronounced it good, God calls upon us to cultivate the world that He created. The magnificent reflection of God within us is the true meaning of work and creativity. The creation of mankind in His image means that we are patterned after Him and are meant to reflect His creative genius and ability to manifest anew.

CASE ILLUSTRATION
Reflecting the Creativity Within

When I walked into the automotive plant in Fremont, California, the first thing I noticed was this statement on the wall:

> CHANGE — to be competitive
> CHALLENGE — to meet the demand
> COMMITMENT — to succeed

Underneath the display was this line: "submitted by team member Katy Cameron." What captured my attention, what made this display extra-special, was that Katy Cameron was not the CEO, vice president, superintendent, manager, supervisor or even team leader in this manufacturing environment. Katy Cameron worked on the assembly line.

In a traditional organization, you would expect to see motivational quotes attributed to the president or CEO. In the lobby of this auto plant, Katy Cameron's name was written in big bold letters where all who entered would see it. This sign tells everyone that the organization respects her contributions as a team member. It says she is valued not only for her work on the assembly line, but also for what she gives of her mind and heart.

POWER TOOLS

Behold, I will do a new thing;
now it shall spring forth;
shall you not know it?
(Isaiah 43:19)

I have shewed thee new things
from this time, even hidden things,
and thou didst not know them.
(Isaiah 48:6)

In the beginning God created
the heavens and the earth. The earth
was without form, and void, and
darkness was on the face of the deep.
(Genesis 1:1-2)

Then God said, Let us make
man in Our image,
according to Our likeness.
(Genesis 1:26)

CONSIDER THE TOPIC OF
"Creativity"

ANSWER THE QUESTIONS BELOW TO ENHANCE
YOUR LEADERSHIP SKILLS.

1. How does this characteristic show up in your life?

_____

_____

_____

2. What is it trying to reveal or teach you? What can you
learn from it? What awareness does it trigger?

_____

_____

_____

3. How might you use this awareness to make positive
changes in your life?

_____

_____

_____

4. Are you willing to live your life differently? In what way?

_____

_____

_____

CHAPTER SEVENTEEN
Encouraging Others

She was giving me "a hard way to go" each day. I knew the situation – or one of us – would not last much longer. We couldn't continue working together under these stressful conditions.

I was about 21 years old, fresh off the college campus of Michigan State University, and recently promoted to supervisor in the production finishing operation of a foundry. Not quite the environment I had envisioned for myself after graduating from college, but a necessary one. I had been told in the graduate-in-training program that I needed to get hands-on — meaning hard-knocks — experience in order to understand the business.

With my degree in labor industrial relations, I thought I'd be negotiating local contracts. Instead, here I was, negotiating day-to-day work assignments on a production line. I made my mind up to hang in and make the best of it. Although all 56 people working on my team were older than me, I knew I had much to learn from them in order to run my operation – I had to gain their trust and learn to trust them as well. Equally important, I had to gain their respect as their supervisor.

Many days were rough. Some workers challenged me because I was so young. One particular employee challenged me daily. She needed medical attention for an illness as soon as the production operation began, or she said needed the restroom but went instead to the cafeteria to play cards. She would frequently come back late from lunch.

As soon as I got the hang of what was going on, I began to address the issues with her, alerting her to the fact that other employees were suffering as a result of her behavior. When the situation progressed to the need for disciplinary action, we were in a constant battle. Each week, there was something revolving around her behavior: discipline, interviews, committee representation, etc.

I wasn't negotiating the contract, but I was learning a lot about labor relations right on the factory floor. I finally penalized this employee to the point of requiring her to spend two weeks at home. Her husband, who also worked at the factory, tried to intervene on her behalf, but his approach was to tell me that I was jealous of her.

When she returned to work, Mary asked if we could be friends.

She said she'd thought about how she had been acting and wanted to apologize and buy my lunch. I declined the lunch, but agreed that I was willing to work with her if she was willing to work with the team.

Over time, her performance and behavior improved, and she asked if perhaps we could get to know each other better outside of work. I shared that over time, certainly we would get to know one another.

ENCOURAGE-MENT IS A VITAL ELEMENT IN LEADERSHIP.

Mary and I often chatted at work. When I initially met her, she was limited by a high school education, was a mother of four, and had a husband who constantly fed her with negative self-images. She told me about her family and how she had always wanted to go to college. I encouraged her, telling her she could be and do anything she wanted, and that as long as she could dream it and see it, she was capable of achieving it.

Eventually, Mary was laid off from the factory, and I ran into her at the mall one day. She again asked if we could be friends and invited me to a gathering at her home. Since she had continued to ask for friendship and I had developed some sense of being able to trust her, I decided to attend.

Through several subsequent interactions over lunch and bowling, I began to understand that this lady was looking for encouragement and a trusting friendship. Mary eventually told me that I had qualities she admired, which is probably why she gave me such a hard time initially.

Today, she has earned a Bachelor's degree and a teaching certificate, and is a very self-confident woman, understanding her worth and value. Her daughter is my goddaughter, and my son is her godson. Most amazing of all, she and I are best friends.

CASE ILLUSTRATION
Share Your Riches

Titus was a Greek whom Paul won to Christ. He became one of Paul's special assistants, and was sent to the churches in Crete as Paul's representative. Paul urged Titus to organize the local churches, and to deal with false teachers.

Paul was a mentor, and an encourager to Titus. He helped to rear him as a follower of Christ who would experience the presence and power of God at work in his life. The role involved active and sometimes daily participation in Titus' life.

Titus had difficulty with the ministry in Crete, and wanted a different assignment. He was working among people who, collectively, had one of the worst reputations in the world at that time. He felt like quitting. But Paul encouraged him to be steadfast in the task, and Titus became successful despite his difficulties.

Do you as a leader encourage others? Encouragement is a vital element in leadership. Sometimes that's all it takes to create a winning force. That simple word or two you say to someone may seem insignificant but can do so much for the soul.

POWER TOOLS

Therefore, encourage one another
and build each other up,
just as in fact you are doing.
(1 Thessalonians 5:11)

Whoever loves his brother lives
in the light, and there is nothing
in him to make him stumble.
(1 John 2:10)

Do not forget to do good and to
share with others, for with
such sacrifices God is pleased.
(Hebrews 13:16)

And let us not grow weary
while doing good, for in
due season, we shall reap
if we do not lose heart.
(Galatians 6:9)

CONSIDER THE TOPIC OF
"Encouraging Others"

ANSWER THE QUESTIONS BELOW TO ENHANCE
YOUR LEADERSHIP SKILLS.

1. How does this characteristic show up in your life?

_____

_____

_____

2. What is it trying to reveal or teach you? What can you
learn from it? What awareness does it trigger?

_____

_____

_____

3. How might you use this awareness to make positive
changes in your life?

_____

_____

_____

4. Are you willing to live your life differently? In what way?

_____

_____

_____

CHAPTER EIGHTEEN
Liberating Others to Win

THE BEST EXECUTIVE IS THE ONE WHO HAS
ENOUGH SENSE TO PICK GOOD PEOPLE TO DO WHAT
HE WANTS DONE AND SELF-RESTRAINT ENOUGH TO KEEP
FROM MEDDLING WITH THEM WHILE THEY DO IT.
Theodore Roosevelt

Self confidence is when we don't have to tear other people down to feel good about ourselves. We must first value who we are before we can value others.

Leaders who are secure in their authority and their ability to be successful are able to encourage their employees to do their best. Rather than micro managing, smart leaders give their employees elbowroom and creative scope. If there are a few tumbles and falls along the way and they're within reason, so what? That is a small price to pay for letting an employee grow on the job.

For people to improve and grow, leaders must give them the room to be creative and the power to influence their work world. Do this, and watch the fires of enthusiasm catch hold and spread. Do this, and you will see how enthusiastically people support what they've helped create.

I once worked with a general manager, who was a great leader. He was always positive, upbeat and unpretentious. He treated people with respect, because he believed in the dignity and worth of each person.

> PEOPLE SUPPORT WHAT THEY'VE HELPED CREATE.

He told me that leaders should look for four elements in their work environment. If these were present, people would make a choice to grow and respond to the demands of the tasks at hand. The four elements are:

1. People should feel that they are *contributing* to the organization.
2. People should be *learning* new and exciting things as they contribute, leading to their continuing growth.
3. People should be *sharing* what they learn with others, helping other people develop.
4. People should have *fun*.

Simple, isn't it? These simple thoughts are why Jerry Collins was seen as a great leader and achieved great results.

Involve employees in decision-making. Provide choices rather than directives. Too often employees are invited to assist with issues that the leader had already decided. It's not a good feeling. However, when you sincerely request employee input and allow people to express their opinions, you win their respect and involvement. When leaders liberate others to be their best, talents emerge.

People won't bust their butts for just anybody or anything. There must be a legitimate reason for enthusiasm. Nine times out of ten, it is the higher purpose of the work being done that makes all the difference in bringing forth the enthusiasm and effort to do the job and do it well.

Establishing an underlying purpose is a way to stay grounded in the midst of a changing world. That higher purpose is going to be different for everyone. Mine is the desire to encourage and help others succeed. It allows me to grow in my abilities to nurture, encourage, motivate and mentor

What is yours?

You, too, have your own unique destiny of how you were meant to contribute. I encourage you to define that for yourself if you haven't already done so. You will find your life enriched and more meaningful.

CASE ILLUSTRATION
Freedom to Win

Nelson Mandela stands as one of the greatest examples of man's ability to triumph over obstacles to liberate others. Mandela headed the black protest against apartheid, the racist policies of South Africa white government. Imprisoned from 1962 to 1990, Mandela became a symbol of the black struggle for racial justice.

In 1991, Mandela was elected President of the African National Congress. He was reelected in 1994, and in his inaugural address said, "Today we are entering a new era for our country and its people. Today we celebrate not the victory of a party but a victory for all the people of South Africa."

Nelson Mandela raised a country from the morass of racism and apartheid to a country of freedom, in unity and purpose.

POWER TOOLS

Let each of you look out not only
for his own interests, but also
for the interest of others.
(Philippians 2:4)

Let no one seek his own, but
each one the other's wellbeing.
(1 Corinthians 10:24)

Because of the service by which
you have proved yourselves,
men will praise God for the
obedience that accompanies
your confession of the gospel
of Christ, and for your
generosity in sharing with
them and with everyone else.
(2 Corinthians 9:13)

CONSIDER THE TOPIC OF
"Liberating Others"

ANSWER THE QUESTIONS BELOW TO ENHANCE
YOUR LEADERSHIP SKILLS.

1. How does this characteristic show up in your life?

_____

_____

_____

2. What is it trying to reveal or teach you? What can you learn from it? What awareness does it trigger?

_____

_____

_____

3. How might you use this awareness to make positive changes in your life?

_____

_____

_____

4. Are you willing to live your life differently? In what way?

_____

_____

_____

CHAPTER NINETEEN
Spirituality at Work

EXCEPT THE LORD BUILDS THE HOUSE
THEY LABOR IN VAIN WHO BUILD IT...
Psalm 127:1 Amp

So why talk about leadership in the context of God, or our spirituality? Because integrating faith with work is nothing new – it has been around since the beginning of time.

While over the years there has been a struggle to integrate spirituality into corporate America, today more than ever there is a groundswell of believers that recognize we can't leave who we are at the door when we enter the corporate corridors. The values we represent follow us – not just to church, but everywhere we go.

INTEGRATING FAITH WITH WORK IS NOTHING NEW

In the aftermath of the terrorist attacks on September 11, 2001, a spiritual revival in the workplace has taken place – or at least, grown more active. Regardless of the reason, people are acknowledging the wholeness of their person rather than shoving their beliefs, values, and spirituality under the desk while they are in the office.

People are organizing employee workplace groups in which they can study the bible, or pray for the health of the company, its products and its leaders. Even though there are traditionalists that would maintain the divide between the secular and the sacred, statistics show that the spiritual revival is here to stay and is active in the workplace.

In 1999, a Gallup survey asked Americans if they believed they needed to experience spiritual growth. At that time, 78 percent of the respondents affirmed that they needed to do so, and 50 percent noted that they spoke of their faith in the workplace. Since the September 11 attacks, employee affinity groups have surfaced at Fortune 500 companies. According to a 2004 Gallup survey, 90 percent of Americans believe in God. When asked if they believed in a "universal spirit," positive responses increased to 95 percent.

Not all of us speak about faith while in the workplace, but when people see the way we act, make decision and serve others, they can be inspired to do the same. Your being an ambassador for the Kingdom of God can occur just in how you choose to show your attributes.

For me, spirituality at work happens daily in how we treat others and the example we set. It is bringing the essence of who we are and what we believe into our work world. Because we spend considerable time at work, what better place is there to exhibit and grow in the qualities of kindness, joy, love and respect? It helps you, it helps the company, and it helps the people you lead.

CASE ILLUSTRATION

Finding Meaning in What we Do at Work Matters

ServiceMaster, a Fortune 500 company with familiar brands such as TruGreen ChemLawn, Merry Maids, American Home Shield, and Terminix generates approximately six billion dollars per year in revenue, and has been known for years for its spiritual culture. ServiceMaster expresses its philosophy in four objectives. The full text is posted on their website, www.servicemaster. com. The objectives are:

Honor God in all we do
      Do the right thing
      Treat each person with dignity and respect
      Respect each person's spirituality
      Protect and maintain our world

Excel with Customers
      Serve others as we would be served
      Make it easy for the customer
      Stand behind our work

Help People Develop
      Help people to do their best every day
      Build proud, dynamic teams
      Help people reach their goals

Grow Profitability
   Act as good stewards of our investors' capital
   Constantly improve and innovate
   Meet our commitments

ServiceMaster's history is built on a strong personal faith and desire to honor God. The leaders of ServiceMaster – founder Marion Wade, Ken Hansen and Ken Wessaer – helped shaped the company as it is today. Their original objectives were stated in this way: "To honor God in all we do; to help people develop, to pursue excellence, and to grow profitability." In 30 years time, only one objective has changed. "Pursue Excellence" was changed to "Excel with Customers." It is no wonder that *Financial Times* ranked ServiceMaster the sixth most respected company in the world in 1998.

In 2006, *Fortune* magazine named ServiceMaster one of America's most admired companies, and *Forbes* named the company one of the 2,000 biggest companies in the world.

POWER TOOLS

Clothe yourselves with compassion,
kindness, humility, gentleness and
patience... over all these virtues
put on love, which binds them
all together in perfect unity.
(Colossians 3:12,14)

If we live in the Spirit,
let us also walk in the Spirit.
(Galatians 5:25)

This I say then, walk in the Spirit and
ye shall not fulfill the lust of the flesh.
(Galatians 5:16)

Seest thou a man diligent in his business?
He shall stand before kings:
he shall not stand before mean men.
(Proverbs 22:29)

CONSIDER THE TOPIC OF
"Spirtuality at Work"

ANSWER THE QUESTIONS BELOW TO ENHANCE
YOUR LEADERSHIP SKILLS.

1. How does this characteristic show up in your life?

_____

_____

_____

2. What is it trying to reveal or teach you? What can you learn from it? What awareness does it trigger?

_____

_____

_____

3. How might you use this awareness to make positive changes in your life?

_____

_____

_____

4. Are you willing to live your life differently? In what way?

_____

_____

_____

CHAPTER TWENTY
The Leader Within

WE MUST BECOME THE CHANGE WE WISH TO SEE.
Mahatma Gandhi

A good leader influences from the heart. Therefore, our hearts must be right in order to be a good leader. In Proverbs 4:23, we are told to guard our heart, for out of the heart springs the issues of life.

Our thoughts, ways, and decisions come from within. It is up to us to move what is inside of us out into the world we inhabit. God gives us the capacity to receive the fruits of the spirit, which are gentleness, faithfulness, goodness, joy, kindness, longsuffering, love, peace, reflection of the character of God, and self control.

THE HEART MUST BE RIGHT TO BE A GOOD LEADER

Too many situations in corporate America today have proven

that leadership has been damaged. Leaders who were once respected have been caught in unethical dealings that ended their careers, and in many cases, their companies. Unfortunately, the negative reputation of these individuals caused employees to question whether leaders can be trusted, especially when they see evidence of similar traits – favoritism, aloofness, incompetence, limited vision, dishonesty, blatant disregard for others, and compromise in their own leadership ranks.

People are flat, unenthused, and do not perform to their highest potential when there is weak leadership. This type of environment causes good employees to seriously search for effective leaders they can follow. Many of today's employers call themselves "an employer of choice," in order to attract the best and brightest of people. The key to attracting and retaining the best is for leaders to demonstrate the characteristics of leadership discussed throughout this book – choosing a winning spirit, enabling others to contribute, recognizing the contribution of each person, inspiring others to victory, integrity, humility, respect for all, fairness, and truth – all of which are within the scriptural "Fruits of the Spirit."

The leader within each of us is different. Authentic leadership comes from what is within our hearts. Our challenge is to find the authentic leader within — each day — despite setbacks, trials and valleys. Like David, one of the most well known biblical figures, we can become leaders others can emulate, inspiring our followers to achieve the impossible. We, ourselves, are not perfect – but we can begin today.

CASE ILLUSTRATION
From Glory, to Glory, to Glory

David the shepherd might never have become king had he worn Saul's armor. He was fully confident, bold, and ready to step out in faith to conquer Goliath, but knew that he would be uncomfortable and unable to win the battle in the heavy armor Saul wanted him to wear. He was authentic in his ways. Although he made mistakes and missteps, he was a man after God's own heart.

Gold, silver and diamonds are not just lying around waiting for us to pick them up. We have to climb mountaintops and dig in caves to find the treasures. The same is true about who we are as individuals. If we continue to dig, we can find our true identity. We will then go from glory to glory, to glory, because the treasures of our leadership skills are within. We can be the leader that God intended us to be. The "best" you that you can be is available. All we can ever hope, ask for, or think, is within our reach. It is a process and a journey, and it is up to each of us to take that journey.

By striving to be as close as possible to God's perfect example, people will be rewarded – because our actions will set a good example to everyone around us. Our leadership behavior starts with us.

POWER TOOLS

But the fruit of the Spirit is love,
joy, peace, longsuffering, gentleness,
goodness, faith, meekness, temperance;
against such there is no law.
(Galatians 5:22-23)

Ye have not chosen Me, but I have
chosen you, and ordained you, that ye
should go and bring forth fruit, and that
fruit should remain: that whatsoever ye
shall ask of the Father in My name,
He may give it you.
(John 15:16)

Behold, I have given him for a
witness to the people, a leader
and commander to the people.
(Isaiah 55:4)

CONSIDER THE TOPIC OF
"Authentic Leadership"

ANSWER THE QUESTIONS BELOW TO ENHANCE
YOUR LEADERSHIP SKILLS.

1. How does this characteristic show up in your life?

_____

_____

_____

2. What is it trying to reveal or teach you? What can you learn from it? What awareness does it trigger?

_____

_____

_____

3. How might you use this awareness to make positive changes in your life?

_____

_____

_____

4. Are you willing to live your life differently? In what way?

_____

_____

_____

Leadership Resources

APPENDICES

Leadership

L eadership is an invisible strand as mysterious as it is powerful. It is a catalyst that creates unity out of disorder. Yet, it defies definition. No combination of talents can guarantee it. No process or training can create it where the spark does not exist.

The qualities of leadership are universal: they are found in the poor and the rich, the humble and the proud, the common man or woman and the brilliant thinker. They are qualities that suggest paradox rather than pattern. But wherever they are found, leadership makes things happen.

The most precious and tangible quality of leadership is trust – the confidence that the one who leads will act in the best interest of those who follow – the assurance that he or she will serve the group without sacrificing the rights of individuals.

Leadership's imperative is a "sense of rightness" – knowing when to advance and when to pause, when to coach and when to praise, how to encourage others to excel. From the Leader's reserves of energy and optimism, his or her followers draw strength. In his or her determination and self-confidence, they find inspiration.

In its highest sense, leadership is integrity. The command by conscience asserts itself more by commitment and example than by directive. Integrity recognizes external obligations, but it needs the quiet voice within, rather than the clamor without.

– Author Unknown

A Leader's Ten Steps to a Winning Spirit

1. Believe in yourself. You are a unique, confident and interesting person – a winner!

2. Don't live with the status quo. Get energized by new ambitions and excitement for living.

3. Challenge the odds and be bold. Free yourself from personal limitations, worry or anxiety.

4. Be open to new ideas and new ways to achieve results. Recognize what others have to share and give.

5. Practice specific leader behaviors. For example, catch people doing things RIGHT, and tell them.

6. Visualize your success. Have definite results in mind.

7. Maintain your focus. You have the power over your thoughts, and you can change your life by changing your attitude.

8. Discipline yourself. Replace inner conflict and doubt with calmness and acceptance of a rich life.

9. Today is the first day of the rest of your life. Enjoy where you are on the path to a new day.

10. Practice being positive and kind. The positive thoughts you send are returned to you.

– Lisa Lindsay Wicker

Quotes from Uncommon Leaders

A leader is best when people barely know he exists, not so good when people obey and acclaim him, worse when they despise him. But of a good leader who talks little when his work is done, his aim fulfilled, they will say: we did it ourselves.

– Lao Tzu

People cannot be managed. Inventories can be managed, but people must be led.

– H. Ross Perot

A good leader inspires others with confidence in him; a great leader inspires them with confidence in themselves.
– Author Unknown

The atmosphere you permit determines the product you permit.

– Mike Murdock

Leaders don't force people to follow – they invite them on a journey.

– Charles S. Laver

The ear of the leader must ring with the voice of the people.

– Woodrow Wilson

There are basically two kinds of leaders: those who sacrifice the people for themselves, and those who sacrifice themselves for the people.

– Rick Joyner

The final test of a leader is that he leaves behind him in other men the conviction and the will to carry on.

– Walter Lippmann

If you want to build a ship, don't herd people together to collect wood. Don't assign them tasks and work. Rather, teach them to long for the endless immensity of the sea.

    — Antoine de Saint-Exupery

The best leaders are apt to be found among those executives who have a strong component of unorthodoxy in their characters. Instead of resisting innovation, they embrace it.

    — David Ogilvy

Leadership is the capacity to translate vision into reality.

    — Warren Bennis

Leadership is lifting a person's vision to higher sights, the raising of a person's performance to a higher standard, the building of a personality beyond its normal limitations.

    — Peter Drucker

Next to the assumption of power is the responsibility of relinquishing it.

    — Benjamin Disraeli

Becoming a manager has much to do with learning the metaphors; becoming a good manager has much to do with using the metaphors; and becoming a leader has much to do with changing the metaphors.

    — Jim Autry

Leadership has a harder job to do than just choose side. It must bring sides together.

    — Jesse Jackson

The growth and development of people is the highest calling of leadership.

    — Harvey S. Firestone

About the Author

*L*isa J. Lindsay Wicker is a Human Resources Executive with a major automotive company in Detroit, Michigan. Internationally recognized as a leader in human resources development and training, Lisa has more than twenty years experience in organizational dynamics and change management.

Lisa formerly served as Corporate Human Resources manager of Employee Enthusiasm Strategies for General Motors North American Operations, and was Vice President of Human Resources for MGM Grand-Detroit – the first African American female to be named to the position in the company's international operations. She also founded Metropolitan Detroit's 101 Best and Brightest Companies to Work For, a program that recognizes companies for valuing employees.

Lisa's accomplishments have earned her recognition as one of the most successful business women in Detroit, by the Detroit News. Her accomplishments include: Former Adjunct Professor at Wayne State University School of Business Administration; Former member of the White House Congressional Forum on Historically Black Colleges and Universities; Recipient of the Career Communications National Woman of Color Professional Achievement Award.

Additionally, Lisa is also a motivational speaker, and has developed a series of tapes on *The Power Inside: Stretch! Discovering the Rewards of Innovation and Risk; and Understanding Your Personal Power.*

For more information on Lisa Lindsay Wicker, speaking engagements, motivational materials, or bulk purchases of this book, contact:

Winning Spirit Ministries

P.O. Box 80145

Rochester, Michigan 48308-0145

Tel: 248.895.1088

Fax: 248.601.0918

EMail: info@the-winningspirit.org

www.the-winningspirit.org

www.ingramcontent.com/pod-product-compliance
Lightning Source LLC
Chambersburg PA
CBHW071227260626
47162CB00004B/1453